Promise to a Guardian Angel

Promise to a Guardian Angel

Ronald Freed and Karin A. Todd

VANTAGE PRESS
New York

This is a work of fiction. Any similarity between the characters appearing herein and any real persons, living or dead, is purely coincidental.

FIRST EDITION

Copyright © 2004 by Ronald Freed and Karin A. Todd

Published by Vantage Press, Inc.
419 Park Ave. South, New York, NY 10016

Manufactured in the United States of America
ISBN: 0-533-14390-X

Library of Congress Catalog Card No.: 2002093336

0 9 8 7 6 5 4 3 2 1

To Ron's mother, Maxine Freed
Who wanted to write a book, but was never able to.
Thank you for your inspiration.

To Karin's mother, Virginia, and daughter, Roxanne:
Always encouraging; always believing.
Thank you, this is for you both.

To all daughters everywhere,
Especially the ones in our lives,
who have such faith in us:
Debra, Marianne, Roxanne, Jessica,
Heather, Jylin, and Teslyn

Acknowledgments

I'd like to take a moment to recognize the support, inspiration, and patience we have received while bringing this book to completion.

To Ron's four grand-nieces—two sets of twins—for providing inspiration for creating the blueprint of our young twin girls.

To Toni Singleton, for her enthusiastic willingness in being the sounding board for the first draft of the story—chapter by chapter as it evolved (minus the last chapter); and her suggestion of (expressed as "hope to see") the further development of the Head Nurse later in the story. Yes, Toni, you finally get to see how it all turns out.

To N. Virginia Todd, for her proofing skills, praise, and suggestions. Next year's birthday will be better, I promise.

To the staff at Vantage Press involved in publishing this book, for their patience in waiting for its return while my life hit one of those turns at 100 mph.

And, last but not least, to my life partner, Pandora, for putting up with the sacrifices endured, and the hours upon weeks upon months upon years (are we into centuries yet?) of staring at my words.

Promise to a Guardian Angel

Part I

Coming Home

1

After a thoroughly enjoyable deep-sea fishing trip in San Diego, Rusty was enjoying the pleasant drive up Highway 101 from San Francisco. He loved this part of California in the spring, with its many mountains, farms, ranches and vineyards. It was peaceful and invigorating with the smell of the cool, clean, fresh air created by the recent storms. Having a 4WD on his Dodge had come in handy quite a few times on the little side trips he had taken, when he had encountered more than one mudslide caused by the storms. He had had great luck on his fishing trip, and had more than enough yellow-fin fish stored in the cooler back in the camper shell of his truck, to be able to give some to his sister, the Judge and Doctor Brown, the long time family physician in Willits.

About twenty miles from Willits he was suddenly hit with an anxiety attack. They didn't happen very often, but when they did, they usually meant something was seriously wrong. His hands and face became icy cold and clammy at the same time, his stomach felt queasy and full of dread. It was as though the Angel of Death had just passed him by. At that moment, Rusty knew his life was about to change—how, remained to be seen.

He began mulling over the possibilities—what might be about to happen? His girlfriend was an operative on assignment in Poland, but her assignments weren't usually as dangerous as the ones he experienced as Sundance (his CIA alter ego). *Sonya just works as a sort of "blender" and obtains tidbits from here and there. Granted, she's very good at it, but that shouldn't put her in the line of any danger. Granted we shouldn't have gotten so involved—if any other operative knew about us, they could use it to their advantage—but we've been discreet. We both knew it wasn't*

3

wise to get too close to anyone in this line of work; but when love comes along, there isn't a whole lot you can do about it. Smokey's given me a couple of months off, so there shouldn't be anything happening in that arena either. I hope nothing has happened up at the ranch; but if it has, I'll know about it soon enough, I'm almost there now. Rusty really hated these premonitions, but they'd saved his life on more than one occasion.

Deciding to pull over for a few minutes and regain his composure, he looked in his rear view mirror and spotted a highway patrol officer with lights blazing. *That's all I need,* he thought, and pulled over to wait for the officer to approach. Looking in his side view mirror, he was a little surprised to see a tall woman, with brown hair and eyes, wearing a CHP uniform approaching. Her body language told him she was all business. *Well, we are almost into the seventies. I'm sure we'll probably see more and more women entering the police workforce—along with every other workforce.*

"May I see your driver's license and registration please?"

Anticipating her request, he had them ready for her and handed them over. She noted that the driver's license was a federal license and that the truck was registered in California. Looking at Rusty, she said, "Both your license and registration need to be from the same state."

"Why don't you read the federal license again," he said patiently, "It states that I am allowed to utilize it in all fifty states."

She looked him over closely and noted the side holster. "Are you carrying any weapons, and if so, what for?" She had one hand at her holster and the other on her radio, signaling for backup.

Rusty grinned and looked at the name on her badge, while he handed her his FBI badge, which he carried in order to keep his CIA identity concealed. "I'll believe you'll find everything in order, Geri. May I call you Geri?"

She looked at both the badge and Rusty at the same time, but kept one hand on her weapon until the backup arrived. Then as another CHP car pulled up she moved away from the door and said, "The name is Officer Abbott, sir. Please step out of the vehicle."

Still grinning, Rusty complied. As the other officer (a man this time) approached, he stated loud enough for him to also hear, "This is a hell of a way to greet a fellow officer of the law, Geri."

"Why were you weaving on the road earlier? Are you on something or have you been drinking?" she asked him.

"I swerved a little to avoid hitting a skunk."

Ignoring his excuse, she looked at him intently, "You look too pale. Are you sure you aren't on something?"

Shaking his head no, Rusty answered her. "I'm just tired. It's been a long drive."

Rusty leaned up against the side of his truck as the two officers talked a while. Geri walked back over to Rusty. "We think you should see a doctor; you look like you need to, and as my mother always says, 'better safe than sorry.' "

"Well, I just happen to be on my way to see Doc Brown in Willits to deliver some fresh fish I caught while deep-sea fishing."

"Really," Geri said with a smile, starting to warm up to him a little, "and what kind of fish did you catch?"

Smiling, he took them both to the back of the truck, and since he had plenty, gave them each one of the fish.

"Thank-you very much," Geri said for both of them. "I think I'll follow you to Doctor Brown's, I'm a little worried about you."

"Fine by me," he said and went to his truck and climbed in.

About fifteen minutes later, they walked into Doctor Brown's office, Rusty set down the box of iced fish, "There's enough for everyone to share," he announced.

As soon as the doctor heard his voice, he was out shaking his hand, "Rusty! It's been entirely too long since the last time I saw you." Noticing Geri standing in the doorway, he included her. "Geri! You too. How are you? Is this guy in trouble already?" Doc Brown was a middle-aged man with silvery gray hair; he was of medium height and weight and had quite a striking personality that fit his profession well.

Geri pulled him aside and quietly spoke to him, "I think you should give him a quick checkup. He doesn't look so good and was swerving on the road."

Doc had Rusty go into an examining room and remove his shirt. Geri followed him in.

"What do you think you're doing?" Rusty asked incredulously.

"I'm concerned and this is part of my job." Geri stood in awe as he stripped to his waist. She couldn't believe any man could have so much muscle, his stomach rippled like a washboard. She also noted the bullet holes and knife scars in various places. "You must get into a lot of dangerous situations as an FBI agent," she stated.

Doc Brown walked in and put his stethoscope to Rusty's chest to listen to his heart while the nurse checked his blood pressure. All seemed to be normal but he still looked a little pale, so Doc took a quick blood sample while he nurse gave him a flu shot. Then the doctor looked him over a little more thoroughly. "You've put on some extra weight since I've seen you."

"Well, I am in my mid-thirties now. I've had to slow down a bit, but I've gained more muscle too, which makes up for the difference."

You've got enough muscle," Doc Brown told him sternly. "You don't need any more."

"I'll try not to," Rusty promised, 'I'm planning to retire soon anyway, and settle down to raise a family."

"Great!" Doc said, "I'll be able to stop recording new scars."

Rusty laughed. "It comes with the territory, Doc," he said. Then turning to include Geri, he continued. "Thanks, both of you, for your concern. I'm gonna head home now." Getting dressed, he went back out to his truck and headed home to his ranch. *It's already been a hell of a day, and not at all as I'd planned. I can't wait to get to the ranch and see what Garth and Sandy have done with the place.*

2

It took him about a half-hour to get to his secluded ranch. He then took out a scan card to open the gate. *It sure feels great to be home.*

As Rusty pulled up to the house, both Garth and Sandy were outside, waiting to greet him. They exchanged hugs, he planted a big kiss on Sandy's head and they walked on into the house. Sandy had made a big pot roast with potatoes and gravy, one of his favorite meals.

"You have got to be the best cook around," Rusty said to her, as he sat back in his chair after cleaning his plate.

"Thanks," she replied, blushing slightly. "I'll get the coffee."

After dinner, Garth and Rusty took their coffee into the living room to talk while Sandy cleaned up the kitchen. Suddenly a buzzer went off, indicating that someone had breached the walls and was on the property. Sandy dropped what she was doing and flipped on the scanner, which showed two blue dots near the main gate. Rusty checked Garth to make sure he had his weapon, and that his 9mm was in its holster. He then reached down and pulled out his .357 for Sandy, "Do you remember how to use this?"

"Of course," she retorted.

Both Garth and Rusty put on headsets and night vision goggles. Garth showed up on the scanner as a gold dot, Rusty as a red dot. This way Sandy would be able to monitor the movement of both the intruders and the interceptors.

Rusty motioned Garth to go up the right side and he took the left, Sandy watched their progress. As they got closer to the main gate, they heard motorcycles. "Are there still only two of the blue dots?" Rusty asked Sandy softly over the radio.

"Yes, and they're coming straight for you."

Overhearing the conversation, Garth went to the other side of the road to give Rusty a hand. With their night vision goggles, they could see both intruders quite clearly. Rusty took the one on the left and Garth the one on the right. Rusty gave his man a huge crushing blow to the head and he dropped like a rock. Garth dropped his target when he struck him just above and behind the right ear with his .357. They dragged both men to the solid oak main gate, picked them up one at a time and threw them over to the other side. Their motorcycles soon followed.

Garth yelled out, "Let this be a warning to you! This is PRIVATE PROPERTY!" They stood there a few minutes until they heard the motorcycles whine out of sight. "This is the first time we've had to use that device," Garth said to Rusty. "It sure works great." They got back to the house and Garth picked up Sandy and whirled her around, saying, "Wasn't that fun?" they then rechecked the monitor, but it was now blank and they turned it off.

"Thanks, both of you," Rusty said.

"Are you kidding?" Garth exclaimed. "I haven't had this much fun in years!"

As Sandy handed Rusty back his .357, he told her, "I want you to have one of these close by at all times from now on. I've made quite a few enemies in my line of work, and I don't want you getting hurt."

"I'll get something," she promised. Rusty gave her a big hug, thanked them both again for their handy work, excused himself and went up to bed.

Part II

Sonya

3

Rusty awoke early the following morning, almost forgetting he was at the ranch. Relishing a hot and invigorating shower, he started thinking of Sonya, and about how great it would be if she were here with him. He was really missing her these days, and couldn't wait for her to finish her assignment in Poland in about two months. Hopefully, she would get a chance to take a vacation and join him here. If not, she only had a little less than a year left of fieldwork to complete; then she would be able to do as she pleased.

Rusty and Sonya had been seeing each other for over six years, and he loved everything about her. They had been so discreet, that Rusty didn't think even Jim Tate, the American Ambassador, knew about their relationship. Rusty had already slipped her an engagement ring, and they planned to be married as soon as she finished her assignment with the Polish government.

Rusty started thinking about how they had met, five years ago, almost to the day. He had just completed an assignment as "Sundance" in Russia. He walked into the American Embassy in Poland to let Jim Tate know he was scheduled for a vacation. He had a very special relationship with Jim and was looking forward to seeing him. Jim was a small, slender man, around forty years of age. He had wavy black hair, a bushy mustache and a big grin (on most occasions). He was from the Deep South and had the type of "Southern Hospitality" commonly associated with the early 1800s. He loved to throw formal parties and could really turn on the charm.

Jim beat him to the punch when they met up. "Ah heah you're slated for a little R & R," he said with a smile.

"How'd you find out about that?" Rusty asked, a little taken aback.

"Oh, Smokey gave me a call. He wants to talk to ya before ya leave here." Jim had a big grin on his face and Rusty knew he'd been had, though wasn't sure just how.

Rusty had an assigned room of his own at the Embassy, since that was his major point of entry into the Soviet Bloc. He went up to this room to give Smokey a call on his secure phone line. "So, I'm back from assignment. Everything went well and I'm ready for my vacation. How's everything been going?"

"Did you talk to Jim?" Smokey asked.

"Yes I did, but he didn't say much."

"Well, Sundance, Jim has a real problem, and I don't have a spare operative at the moment, to see what's coming down. He's been followed, has been for about a week, and it really has him worried."

"Hell, he has ump-teen Marines around to guard him; what the hell does he need me for?" Rusty asked. He was watching his dream of a quiet vacation fade away.

"I think it's a foreign operative, and I told him I'd have you check it out—just to be on the safe side." Smokey told him, "By the way, he's throwing a party tonight at the Embassy; you should be there."

Unable to see Smokey's grin on the other side of the phone, Rusty swore, "Oh shit, I hate having to dress up for these damn functions. All right, I'll take the assignment; but I want my vacation as soon as I'm done with it."

Smokey thanked him and hung up.

Rusty went downstairs in search of Jim Tate. Upon finding him, he stated, "I don't have a tux here, so I'm going to have to wear one of my regular suits to tonight's shindig."

Jim smiled and responded, "Check your closet. I took the liberty of gettin' ya one. I took one of your suits to my tailor, and had a tuxedo made to your size." Seeing Rusty's scowl, Jim laughed and said, "Hell, Sundance, y'all probably have all the pretty gals running after ya for being so handsome! Just try to have some fun."

"Yeah right," groaned Rusty. "Sure I will."

Having decided to check out the Embassy to make sure all the bases were covered, Rusty told Jim to meet him an hour before everyone started arriving, and to have all of his Marine officers attend the function in tuxedos as well. Bewildered, Jim said he would see to it.

Rusty checked out all the exits and entrances. He then spoke to the Gunnery Sergeant to assign two Marines to be at each critical area at all times, making sure everyone only used the front exits and to insure no one was able to enter any restricted areas. Two marines were to act as relief, allowing for frequent breaks keeping the men alert, without compromising security. After receiving the Gunnery Sergeant's assurance that all would be taken care of, Rusty went back to his room for a quick nap.

4

It was about 6:00 P.M. and the party would be starting around 7:30. Rusty had finished showering and had just put his tux on, discretely securing his weapons, when there was a knock on his door. "Come on in, Jim," he said.

"You're lookin' sharp." Jim said, "The gals are goin' to be all ovah ya tonight."

"Thanks. Oh, by the way," Rusty said, "I've posted all your Marines where I want them, so don't pull them away from their posts."

"Hey, wait a minute; those are my men!"

Rusty smiled, "Do you want your shadow to be taken care of, or not? I'm not the one being followed around. I'd love to just leave this up to you and your Marines and go on vacation, but Smokey has asked me to handle this. If it turns out to be someone serious, it's my job to protect you—at all costs. To do this I need to handle the security procedures. Don't worry, this is what I'm good at."

Grumbling under his breath, Jim agreed not to interfere.

Walking down the corridor towards the main reception room, Rusty asked, "So, how many officers do you have in civilian dress?"

"Three—that's all the tuxedos I could get on such short notice."

"That should be enough. Make sure you have at least one of them at your side at all times."

Looking at Rusty, Jim stated, "Ya don't take many chances, do ya?"

"That's my job, and I don't like loose ends. Try to act casual

14

tonight. If you spot your shadow, let me know as soon as you can, without being obvious."

"Ah'll do that."

Everything was now set for the drama to unfold. The Embassy guests and other VIPs were starting to trickle in. When the East German Embassy started entering the ballroom, he spotted someone he was sure would turn out to be Jim's shadow. He was one of the East German operatives, who was tough and had a mean and nasty temper. Something Smokey had told him long ago, "Once you let your emotions interfere with your judgment, you lose your edge."

Rusty walked nonchalantly to Jim; "I think I've spotted him. Is that him right over there?" When Jim nodded in confirmation, he continued, "His code name is `The Baron' and he is one hell of an asshole to deal with. Do you have something on him? Or did you just tick him off somehow?"

Jim grinned a little, "Well, ah was at a restaurant the other night, with a young lady, and accidentally bumped into him. He got real upset and ah apologized, but that didn't seem to be enough and so two of my escort Marines jumped between us until the guy backed off, goin' on his way."

"You don't know how lucky you are," Rusty told him, "if he had really wanted to, he could have taken out you and both of your Marines in about two minutes. He's that good." He saw Jim's face start to turn white, and hurried to reassure him, "He won't try anything here. He's just letting you know he hasn't forgotten."

"What should ah do?"

"Absolutely nothing," Rusty said. "From now on, he's mine. Make sure that none of your Marines try anything stupid; they probably wouldn't live long enough to tell you about it."

"What are ya goin' to do?"

"Don't worry about that. Its just business as usual. I'll just make sure he knows he's unwelcome. He should be gone in about a half-hour. He won't want to make a scene and he doesn't particu-

15

larly want to mess with me either. He's damn good, and makes one hell of an adversary, but he knows he'd probably lose if it comes down to either him or me. He already knows I'm here and is probably waiting to see what I have in mind."

Walking casually, Rusty approached The Baron, and bumped him lightly as he went by. He was a large man with blonde hair and mean-looking eyes. He looked at Rusty and asked, "What's your problem?"

Looking back at him, Rusty replied, "Stay away from the Ambassador, or you'll be seeing Hell a whole lot sooner than you anticipated. If you have a problem, you deal with me."

"Well, if he couldn't handle this himself, he shouldn't have pissed me off, then he wouldn't be having this problem."

"This is a diplomatic function. I want you to vacate these premises within half an hour, without causing any problems. If you want, I'll meet up with you later and we can settle this."

The Baron agreed, "You two don't have too much more time to live."

Rusty smiled and said, "As long as you go through me first."

"No problem."

Returning to the party to find Jim, Rusty spotted a young lady dressed in an evening dress of light blue suede with rhinestone swirls. The hem was just above the knee. She had shoulder length, sandy colored hair and the most beautiful emerald green eyes he'd ever seen. Her nose was petite and her mouth was fantastic, especially when she smiled, her lips had that cute pouting sort of look that was just delicious. She was of medium height and had one hell of a sensual body. Turning toward her, he could hardly take his eyes off of her. When he bumped into another couple, he turned about three shades of red and apologized to them. By this time Jim and the beauty were both watching him and laughing.

Walking up to them, Rusty asked Jim, "Who is this gorgeous lady?"

Jim said, "Trust you to zone in on the prettiest filly here! This beautiful young lady is Sonya."

"Just Sonya!" asked Rusty.

"That's all you need to know," quipped Sonya. "You must be Sundance. I've heard a lot about you. Is all of it true?"

"Yes, I'm Sundance, and that's all you need to know," he returned.

Sonya laughed, "Well, I guess I asked for that one."

"So, what line of work are you in?" Rusty asked her.

Jim, answering for her stated, "She's in the same field you are, except in a lighter capacity."

Wondering what he meant by that, Rusty made a mental note to ask Jim about it later.

"So, I saw you talking to The Baron earlier," Sonya said, "he is one mean individual, I hope you are being extremely careful there."

"Yes, I know. He has a very mean and vengeful temper. That temper will probably get him terminated someday soon."

"A lot of operatives have tried that and ended up being on the losing end instead," Sonya mentioned.

Rusty just smiled and stated, "I can handle that problem if it comes down to it. Would you excuse us a moment?" Taking Jim off to the side, he said, "We have a real problem here, we'll need to discuss it later, after the party."

Then, speaking to the Marine officer accompanying Jim, "The Baron is getting ready to leave, make sure you follow him off the premises. Don't get into any confrontations with him; he's deadly and way out of your league. If there's a problem, send for me immediately."

Promising to see to it, the officer left. Rusty kept a close eye on The Baron, and as he started to depart, Rusty made sure he stayed between him and Jim until he was out of sight. He didn't expect any problems at this time, but better to make sure nothing out of the ordinary happened, as The Baron could be unpredictable.

17

Rusty then returned back to Sonya, and was stunned again by her smile.

She asked, "What was that all about?"

"Nothing serious," he assured her, "the situation is well under control."

The orchestra was playing a nice slow song; taking her hand, Rusty led her out to the dance floor. He felt an electric sensation shoot through him as he took her into his arms and began to dance. "You look stunning tonight," he told her. "Is there anyone I need to worry about?"

Blushing, she replied, "No. In my line of work it is very difficult to develop a steady relationship."

"I know exactly what you mean," he said. He then held her closer to his chest and they just danced, moving together smoothly.

The dance ended and Rusty walked her over to the table Jim had managed to procure for them. Jim, with cocky half grin on his face said, "Ah told ya there would be some pretty girls here. Ah'm glad to see you've taken my advice and started to enjoy yo'self."

"You didn't tell me they would be this pretty," Rusty retorted. Sonya began blushing again.

"Well, ah guess ah'll leave the two of you alone, ah have a lot of other guests ah need to greet."

After the party, Rusty offered to take Sonya home. She agreed and said, "Let's walk. I'm less than a mile away, and it's such a beautiful warm summer night."

Rusty had never felt like this before. He had had plenty of other relationships, but none of those women had made him feel this way. He wondered if he was finally falling in love. If so, it sure felt great!

When they reached her front door, she said, "I'd ask you in but this is our first date."

Grinning, Rusty grabbed the opportunity and said, "Well, if this is our first date, I guess I'm going to need to get your phone number, to make sure we get a second one." Then he drew her close and gave here a tender kiss.

Leaving his arms reluctantly, she said, "I do have the day after tomorrow open, if you're interested."

Squeezing her hand gently, Rusty said, "I'll pick you up around ten in the morning."

"It's a date." She then opened the front door, quickly walked in, and softly closed it behind her.

Rusty was on cloud nine all the way back to the Embassy.

5

The following morning, Rusty got up, had a quick workout with the weights and went back to his room for a hot shower. He had already called Smokey and relayed the events of last night to him. He then started digging for as much intelligence about the Baron as he could get, so he would know just what he was dealing with. Smokey gave him all he had and then told him to be extremely careful, as the Baron was one mean operative. Rusty had said he would. He was relaxing with a strong cup of coffee when Jim called, asking him to come down to talk. Telling Jim he would be down in a few minutes, he started getting dressed.

Arriving in the dining room, he saw that Jim had already started eating breakfast. "Sit down," he said. "Yours is on the way." It arrived as Rusty was taking his seat, and both men fell into silence until they finished their meals.

Jim was looking a little tired and worried. "Relax," Rusty told him, "I've got everything under control."

"Are ya sure ah don't have ta worry 'bout him coming aftah me?"

"I have his promise that he will deal with me first, and if nothing else, he does keep his promises. He takes pride in his honor, and wouldn't want to tarnish his credibility, which would put him in a bad light with the East German Hierarchy as well."

"I spoke ta Smokey," Jim stated. "He says this guy is a verrry dangerous man."

"Well, so am I," Rusty replied. "I've taken care of more sinister operatives than him over the years. He had a run-in with a Soviet operative, the Black Raven, a couple of years ago, and didn't do so well. The Black Raven and I are about on the same level.

Someday we'll have to find out who's better. It will probably be quite a fight. Anyway, back to the Baron—stop worrying about him."

"When do ya expect to meet up with the Baron?" Jim asked.

"Soon, real soon."

"How did you and Sonya do last night?" Jim asked, with a sly grin.

"Oh, we got along fine," Rusty said blandly. "We'll probably see each other again, but I don't want to get to close. I wouldn't want to endanger her life."

"Ya know, she's got 'bout seven more years here in Poland. It's her paycheck for them sending her ta college."

"No hurry," Rusty said. "If anything does happen, we've got those seven years to find out about each other. If we end up wanting something any sooner, my dad's inventions have made me a millionaire in my own right, and I could probably buy off her Polish commitment if we wanted to. We'll see how it goes. I'm in no hurry to rush things, and her safety is paramount."

"Just treat her right," Jim said, "she's truly a wonderful lady."

"You've sure got that right. Now, if you'll excuse me, I have a few things to take care of. And stop worrying so much, you're going to give yourself a stroke!"

Going back to his room, Rusty started mulling things over and decided, if at all possible, this night would be a good one for the assassination. It would be very dark, and he could use the practice on his stealth procedures. Stealth was one of his strong points, but you need to keep using it if you want to keep it. During his fifteen years as an operative, Sundance had four major weapons at his disposal. First was a 9mm carried in a shoulder holster. His second weapon was a small gas type pistol that shot small poison darts. The darts would penetrate the victim and dissolve. Within thirty seconds the victim would be dead of a massive heart attack and no one would be any the wiser as to how the victim had died. This method had kept him out of a lot of trouble over the years. His

21

next choice was a ten-inch switchblade that was well hidden in his belt and his last major weapon was a four-inch .38 police special placed in an ankle holster.

Pulling out his folder on the Baron, he started looking it over to discover what weapons he was likely to come up against, and what the Baron's strengths and weaknesses were. According to the file, the Baron's primary weapon was a knife. If that didn't do the job, he would probably go for his German luger, with which he was extremely accurate. He noted that their height was about even, his weight was about 240 pounds and he was right-handed. Rusty realized that the indications were that the Baron would have the advantage in speed, but he would have the advantage in power. He would need to keep these things in mind when he made his move. He would also be able to use the Baron's temper against him, if he needed to.

Checking out the Baron's haunts, he tried to figure out where the best place for the encounter would be. It needed to be somewhere dark and out of the way. He then checked his weapons, making sure they were in top working order. With his homework done, he was now ready; all he had to do was relax and wait for night to fall.

Rusty lay back on the bed and began thinking of Sonya. He hadn't been able to get her out of his mind, and was looking forward to seeing her again. Then he started blocking his thoughts of her, in order to prepare for his meeting with the Baron. He didn't need any distractions tonight.

He didn't want Jim to know what was going on or when, as this mission was his to do alone. The last thing he needed was someone playing hero and getting in his way, while attempting to "help." He would leave a message that he was out with some old friends.

6

It was eleven o'clock and the evening was dark with overcast skies. Sundance had gotten in a nice long nap, and now felt fresh, with all of his faculties in order. He casually strolled out of the Embassy and got into his car. He knew the Baron could soon be walking home from his favorite tavern, so he drove in that direction. Finding a parking place, he got out and started looking for a secluded place near the tavern. He found one that would be perfect for their encounter.

A couple of hours later, the Baron came out of the tavern and headed his way. Sundance waited patiently until he was within arm's length of him. He then stepped out of the dark, taking the Baron by surprise; but within a split second the Baron had his knife out and had put a deep gash on Sundance's right arm. Being left-handed, he was able to put the pain out of his mind and continue. Sundance countered with a powerful left to the Baron's temple. The Baron then staggered back about five feet and went for his luger, but this time Sundance was ahead of him and put a poison dart from his gas pistol into the Baron's neck. The Baron got off one shot, just missing Sundance's head, and it was over. Sundance quickly got all of the Baron's weapons and other personal items, so he could send them to Smokey in a courier pouch. From this information, the CIA would gain valuable clues about how the East Germans worked.

He then silently walked away in the dark, got into his car and disappeared into the night. He thought to himself, *A masterpiece well done, it took less than two minutes, and not a sound was uttered to draw attention. That puts an end to innocents being executed by that operative due to his nasty temper.*

23

Rusty walked into the American Embassy around three in the morning and was surprised to see Jim was still up. He looked at Rusty and said, "Well?"

"Well what?"

"Sundance, don't give me any 'Well what?' Did ya get him?"

"What makes you think I went after him tonight?"

"Your d'meanor gave you away when ya left this evenin'."

"I guess I'll have to watch that a little more closely," Rusty said.

Jim then saw the blood coming down Rusty's arm and hand. "Ah think we need to get ya to the dispensary and have that wound checked out."

On the way, Rusty started relating what had happened. He could see the relief on Jim's face, once he realized it was all over. "I have some items that must go into the next courier pouch earmarked for Smokey."

"Ah'll take care of it myself," said Jim.

They arrived in the dispensary, and the doctor was waiting for them. Rusty needed thirty-seven stitches from that little adventure. Jim decided that as glamorous as it may sometimes seem, he could do without adventure after all. After being assured that Rusty's last tetanus shot was current, the doctor gave him some mild pain relievers and antibiotics. Rusty then thanked the doctor, excused himself and went straight to his room.

Calling Smokey as soon as he reached his room, he told him what had happened and what he'd be receiving in the next courier pouch. "Now I'm going on a month's vacation, and I don't want you interrupting it."

"You deserve it," Smokey replied. "Enjoy."

Rusty set his alarm for eight in the morning so he wouldn't be late for his date with Sonya. He then fell into the sleep of the dead.

7

The alarm went off, and Rusty dragged himself out of his drug-induced sleep. His arm throbbed like hell. Shaking it all off, he took a pain reliever, went in to take a steaming hot shower, shaved and put on some expensive aftershave. The pain medication started to work and the shower felt great. He got dressed and went to the dining room for a quick breakfast of coffee and sweet rolls.

He arrived at Sonya's at five minutes to ten. She invited him in to wait for her while she finished getting ready. He took a quick glance around her flat. It was a nice clean little home with one bedroom. It was comfortably furnished with a huge couch that Rusty loved—it would even fit his large frame. Sonya came back out, she was wearing a light green blouse with tan slacks and she looked stunning. Rusty reached over and gave her a light kiss. She fixed him a cup of coffee and said she would be finished in a few minutes. He heard a grandfather clock strike ten, and thoroughly enjoyed the sound of it. It reminded him of the one in his parents' home when he was very young.

Sonya walked in just then and saw him looking to be miles away. She took a moment to take in the picture of him. He was a tall, well built man in his mid-thirties. His easily 6'3" frame was complemented with ninety pounds of muscle. He was a big boned man, with a massive, well-muscled chest and shoulders, huge arms and large hands. His waist slimmed down to about forty inches and he had long, strong legs. His face was tanned and weathered, and middle age was trying to creep in. He had dark brown wavy hair, an average nose and a square jaw. His sensuous mouth would smile wide, creating a dimple in his left cheek when he was enjoying himself. His smoldering dark blue eyes were his biggest assets. When he pinned you under his stare, you would swear he could read your innermost thoughts. He was quite a handsome devil, in a rugged sort of way. While jeans, t-shirt and boots were what he seemed to be most comfortable in, she saw last night that he could wear formal attire and blend into society with no problem, when he chose.

"Where are you right now?" she asked as she sat down on the couch beside him.

"Your grandfather clock bought to mind a childhood memory, that's all."

"Tell me about your childhood and how you came to be the man you are," she said. "I want to know all about you."

With that, Rusty settled in to give as much of a summary of his life as he was allowed. "Well, I spent my early years in a mountain resort in Southern California. My parents were killed in a tragic aircraft accident while they were coming back from obtaining a patch for a laser device used for security purposes. This invention would let you know if anyone trespassing was on your property and would also let you know exactly where the intruders were at all times. Both the CIA and FBI were keenly interested in this device.

"A judge and his wife took me in. I was about fifteen, and they raised me as the son they'd never had. Their only child, Barbara, was also fifteen and we got along famously, so I was able to fit right in with the family. The judge trained me in the art of boxing and weightlifting, which I thoroughly enjoyed. He and I became very close and when I excelled in school, he sent me to university to study law.

"The judge was a federal judge and was able to arrange for me to go through the FBI training course after I graduated university. I completed the course with honors but didn't feel that it was quite my cup of tea—something was still missing. I wanted more adventure.

"When the assignments came out for the new recruits, my name didn't appear and since I had done so well, I was puzzled. I went to see the director. I knocked on the door and was told to enter. He had me sit down and explained that he thought there was something else I would be interested in that was more exciting than one of the normal assignments given to the new recruits.

"He pushed a buzzer, and an older gentleman walked in. He was neatly dressed and had an air that showed he had experienced a lot in his lifetime. He had the kind of assurance that I wanted to have when I was his age. He looked me over and then looked through his files briefly. Then he smiled at me and asked if I would like to join the CIA. It could be quite an exciting but dangerous path, so I would have to learn how to walk a very fine line.

"Needless to say, I was all for it and grinned back, telling him that that sounded exactly like what I wanted to do with my life. Then he said he'd see me later and left. The director gave me an address and a date to get started. I would later find out that the other gentleman's code name was Smokey, and that he would be my boss and give me my assignments in the future. No other information was divulged to me.

"After I finished my CIA training course, I became a specialized agent and assassin, and would slip in past the iron curtain on covert missions, bringing others out of trouble and into friendly territories. The code name I was given is Sundance and after nine years, if I do say so myself, I have built up quite a reputation. So there you have it—the life and times of Sundance."

"Glad to meet you, Sundance. Would you care to take in the sights of Warsaw with me now?"

Sonya took him to visit some of the museums and other scenic places; then they went to lunch. While they were eating and engaging in small talk, Rusty could hardly take his eyes off of Sonya. She was radiant. After the meal they went to the local park. It was beautiful, as was the day. The sun was shining warmly, and the birds were enjoying it as much as they were. He loved holding her hand as they strolled by the lake, stealing a kiss now and then; and she was adorable when she pointed out things she wanted him to see.

Sonya found Rusty to be a very handsome and powerful man with a fantastic personality. She could sense the chemistry between them. She almost felt like a school girl on her first date. She watched the big man take everything in; he didn't seem to miss anything. When she had grabbed onto his right arm as they started walking, she noticed that he grimaced a little, he didn't say anything, so neither did she; but she couldn't help wondering about it.

It had been a wonderful afternoon and now the sun was headed down. It was almost seven o'clock, and they decided to go to dinner. The swordfish was delicately browned, the mashed potatoes were flavored with garlic and the asparagus spears were perfect. They polished off the wonderful meal and headed out to his car. As Sonya touched Rusty's right arm, she saw his face tighten up again. "So when are you going to tell me what happened to your arm?"

"Oh it's nothing, I must have twisted it a little."

She frowned at him. "Sundance, I really want to know what happened."

Rusty gave in and told her about the demise of the Baron.

"Why didn't you tell me sooner?"

"You didn't ask."

"How bad is the wound?"

"I had to have a few stitches," Rusty said nonchalantly.

"Well, the Baron was a hell of a nasty individual, you've done the world a big favor, getting rid of him. I want to take a look at that wound when we get back to my place. We don't want it getting infected."

"Okay, but you worry too much. The doctor has given me antibiotics to fight off any infection."

When they walked into Sonya's flat, she immediately sat him down on a dining room chair. "Take off your jacket and shirt," she said as she went into the kitchen to start some coffee. When she returned, she took the bandage off. It was bleeding lightly, so she rinsed it off with hydrogen peroxide. She then put some type of ointment on it and replaced the bandage. Laughing, she said, "The next time you're hurting this bad, we'll stay home. Do you have any pain medication?"

"Yes."

"I want you to take two pills now, plus this," and she handed him another pill.

"What's this?"

"It's a mild sedative. Sleep will help that arm heal more rapidly." She reached up to touch his forehead, "You're also running a slight fever, have you been keeping up on taking those antibiotics?"

"Yes, dear," he said, and laughed, as she scowled at him playfully.

Going to the linen closet for a sheet, blanket and pillows, Sonya made up the big, overstuffed couch Rusty had been eyeing earlier that morning. "Put your weapons on the coffee table and crawl in." When he had complied, she removed his shoes, and spotting his .357 magnum, removed that as well, placing it with the other weapons. Looking at them all, she laughed, "You could probably fight off a whole army, all by yourself."

Looking back at her, he winked and solemnly stated, "A man must have his toys." A few minutes later, he was out like a light. Sonya stayed with him for about an hour, just gazing at his handsome face, his dark brown wavy hair, and realized that she was already in love with this big guy. It had happened so fast, she couldn't believe it.

8

The next morning, Rusty woke up early. He stretched out his arm, and it felt much better. Whatever that ointment was that Sonya had used, it was fantastic. He would have to be sure to find out about it and add it to his emergency kit.

Going out to his car, he grabbed the overnight case he always had with him, and pulled out a clean shirt. He went into the bathroom to clean up; then went into the kitchen to make breakfast. He started the coffee and then cooked up some flapjacks, bacon and eggs. Everything smelled delicious. He was getting ready to take some in to Sonya, when he turned around and saw her standing in the doorway. She was wearing her bathrobe and her hair was a little wild, looking at her, he fell in love with her all over again.

"And he cooks!" she exclaimed, feigning exaggerated disbelief. "You're just full of surprises, aren't you?"

He walked over, gave her a kiss, and said, "Breakfast is ready."

Neither one of them could take their eyes off the other while they ate breakfast and engaged in small talk. Rusty knew the sparks would be flying shortly. Sonya led him to the bedroom and Rusty slowly seduced her. He loved her fantastic body. Neither of them got out of the bed the whole day, unless it was necessary. Rusty discovered that being in love with the woman you are making love to, enhances the experience a thousand fold. It was the most wonderful day of his life.

They spent the rest of the month together, enjoying each other's company both in and out of the bedroom. At the end of the month, during a candlelit dinner, Rusty pulled out a beautiful engagement ring, "Will you marry me?"

With tears in her eyes she said, "I can't right now. I still have a seven-year contract with the Polish government, and while I'm honoring that contract, I'm not allowed to get married."

"Keep the ring, I'll wait those seven years for you. We'll see each other as often as possible without letting on to anyone that we'll be together."

Still crying, she said, "I'll keep it, and we will be married the day my contract ends. I love you more than life itself."

For the next five years, they became more and more deeply in love, and cherished every moment they were able to have, and prayed that no one had yet found them out.

Part III

End of a Dream

9

Snapping back to reality, Rusty remembered he was in California on his ranch. As he headed for the kitchen, he thought, *Only one more year, and we can get married!* That thought put a big smile on his face.

As he approached the dining room and kitchen, he could smell breakfast cooking. He entered, said hi to both Garth and Sandy, and poured himself a big cup of hot coffee. He drank in the strong aroma while letting the steam heat up his face. Breakfast was superb. Rusty thought to himself, *There's nothing like a cold crisp morning in the mountains to sharpen your appetite.*

After breakfast, the three of them took a stroll around the ranch. Garth and Sandy took pleasure in showing Rusty everything that had been done since he had been here last. Rusty loved his ranch and thoroughly enjoyed spending time there. He thought back to when he first came to this ranch.

Judge Hardaway's family had resided in Southern California when Rusty first went to live with them, but the judge had later been transferred to the San Francisco area. He had purchased the ranch, which was just off of Highway 20. It was surrounded by an impenetrable forest of redwoods, providing absolute privacy. It was fifty-six acres, and was complemented by a big beautiful lake. There was a large mountain that butted up against the lake, making it almost inaccessible. There was only one way to get to the lake—the trail from the house. Any other attempt would prove to be too much of a climb with too many obstacles in the way.

He had put a rock wall around the property for privacy. The wall had rod iron spikes cemented to the top, to keep out trespassers. In the center of the ranch, he built a beautiful four-bedroom home with all the amenities. He also built three smaller one bed-room cottages for visitors.

The judge had really enjoyed the property until his wife died, at which time he moved to San Francisco in order to be closer to his daughter who now lived in Sonoma. He gave Rusty the ranch to do with as he liked. The ranch was a blessing for Rusty as he made many enemies during his fifteen years with the CIA, and would make a few more before either being killed or retiring, whichever came first. He really cherished the property, and loved the solitude.

He had made some improvements to the property. There was now a dock and boathouse at the lake, at which he stored all his fishing gear. He had also added four more cottages. For security purposes he installed his father's invention, which would let him know immediately of any prowlers.

Garth Tanner was a retired agent with the CIA. He had a bad leg, which never healed properly and had forced him into early re-tirement. Garth, a rough-looking man in his early thirties, was still a menacing figure; a tall blonde man that reminded you of an early viking warrior. He was the strong silent type and had a pleasant smile, with light blue eyes that sparkled. He had brought his wife Sandy, an attractive, petite lady with light brown, shoulder-length hair, pretty green eyes and a warm smile with him when he came to the ranch. They occupied one of the small cottages and looked af-ter the ranch as caretakers. They were a very loving couple and loved being there.

While Rusty had been gone, Garth had done a great job on the now seven guest cottages. He had refurbished and painted them, and they blended in with the forest so well, you almost didn't see them while looking right at them.

Heading down to the lake, Rusty said, "I really should try my hand at fishing there sometime soon. I bet those fish are getting mighty big."

Garth and Sandy laughed. "We've caught a few nice ones,"

Garth said. "Some large catfish, a few small mouth bass and trout, and even a couple of sunfish."

"I guess I'll have to do that this summer," Rusty said enviously. As they arrived at the lake, he noticed that Garth had also refurbished the dock and boathouse. They looked great. "You've done a fantastic job with the place, Garth."

Beaming, Garth replied, "I enjoy it."

Rusty had plans for putting in four modular homes as well. One for the judge when he retired, one for his sister, Barbara, for when she and her family dropped in to visit, one for Garth and Sandy to have for their own use once he retired and started spending more time at home. The other one would be for guests who would be staying for longer than a month. This would leave the guest cottages open for guests that were staying for no more than a few days.

Garth had put in a new blacktop road from the main gate to the main house, to the cottages and on to the boathouse. In the middle of the road was a huge oak tree that Rusty really loved. Garth had created an island in the blacktop to honor its majesty. The gate was about 500 feet from the main house and cottages. This gave a feeling of total seclusion that Rusty appreciated. When the judge had given him this piece of land, he hadn't realized how much he would come to appreciate the peace and serenity it would offer him in the future. He had lots of other plans for it, but they were pie in the sky dreams, and would require time and patience.

The property was filled with a scattering of pine, oak and giant, massive redwood trees. Some of them were hundreds of years old. He was glad to know that no one would be able to chop down these trees. They were his. The wild life was abundant with squirrels, raccoons, opossums, deer, and occasional coyotes, bobcats, and mountain lions. If it weren't for the big stone wall that completely surrounded the property, it would be easy to get lost here. He had the feeling that this wilderness was a special piece of God's country and that it was almost too beautiful. One could come out here, be very still, start breathing with the earth and be at peace.

Seeing Rusty deep in thought, Garth knew exactly how he was feeling. He and Sandy also loved this land and would stay here for as long as Rusty would let them.

Rusty then looked at Sandy and Garth and started telling them about his plans for the modular houses, including the one that would be for Garth, Sandy and their future family. "Go ahead and pick out the spot you want it to be." Both of them were caught off guard and thanked him for is generosity, as they both loved the ranch so much.

"It will probably be a couple more years before I retire and we start making it a reality, but it is time to start thinking about these plans."

"Thank God you are starting to think of retiring. You are so lucky to have gone this far without getting seriously hurt or killed," Garth exclaimed.

"I've thought about that. I'm also beginning to get tired of the constant roaming. I want to settle down and relax while I'm still young enough to do it. Especially now."

Garth and Sandy looked at each other speculatively, but let the comment pass for now. Looking around, Rusty felt that the property almost had a medieval look about it, with the massive trees and the moss hanging from the branches. He decided to himself that once he and Sonya were married, he would love to have some children roaming around this place. It would make it just perfect. Looking up at the big oak tree, he thought to himself, *I could build a huge treehouse in this tree for my kids to enjoy. I could also hang some swings from that big branch over there, and install a big slide from the one over there. Sonya is going to love this place. I can't wait to have her here with me. We'll have this ranch forever.* Looking back at the lake, he thought, *I can't wait to teach my son or daughter to fish in that lake.*

Suddenly Sandy interrupted his thoughts. "Hey you," she said. "Where'd you go?"

"Oh, I'm just having dreams about the future."

Sandy gave him a studied look. Deciding to broach him later on the subject, she kept her silence. They headed back up to the house, and Sandy poured them some more coffee and then tidied up the kitchen. When she was done, she joined them in the living room. Garth had started a fire in the fireplace, and the room was getting toasty warm.

The three of them sat around, enjoying the fire and talking about the future. Then Sandy asked, "So Rusty how's your love life?"

"Well, I'm figurin' on getting married in a couple of years."

Sandy smirked and nodded while Garth looked at her with raised eyebrows and then back at Rusty. "Congratulations! Who's the lucky girl?" Garth asked while thinking to himself, *Boy, Sandy sure called that one.*

"You'll know in time," and he wouldn't say another word about it.

The phone rang and Garth went to answer it. Sandy was looking at Rusty quizzically and was about to say something more, but Garth came back in, "Smokey wants to talk to you."

Swearing under his breath, Rusty went to the phone. "The party to whom you wish to speak is not available to take your call. Please leave a message at the sound of the beep."

"Nice try, Sundance, but I have to cut your vacation short. I have an extremely urgent assignment for you; but you should be home well before Christmas. You have a flight out of Oakland in about six hours. It is scheduled to take off at four-fifteen. A car will be waiting for you at the airport."

Rusty hurried up to his room to pack. The tone in Smokey's voice led him to believe the situation was extremely serious. Outside by the truck, he gave both Garth and Sandy big hugs. Sandy handed him a lunch to eat on the way. "Thanks, I'll be home soon." He got in the truck and took off.

10

Ten hours later, he was sitting in Smokey's office. Smokey walked in. "Great timing," he said. Rusty started to stand up. "Sit back down. Here's the situation: do you remember 'the Wasp'?"

"Yes; I worked with him on a couple of occasions. He seemed to be an efficient operative. Why?"

"It appears he's defected," Smokey answered. "I was giving him some important items to be taken to another agent, when my secretary called me out for a moment. When I got back, he was acting a little strange, but I was worried about another situation that was developing, so I didn't think too much about it.

"Later, the agent he was supposed to give the items to turned up dead, and we didn't hear from him. On a hunch, I played the video from my office back from the time that he was in there alone and saw him going through the folder on my desk, he slipped out a sheet of paper and stuck it in his pocket, before I came back in. When I double-checked that folder, I discovered the list of ten of my special agents and their locations was missing. I have contacted them all to reassign them to other locations for now.

"I found out he sold the list for one million American dollars to the Russians, but it will take a few days to finish the transaction. After that, he'll have to find a way down to Warsaw, so he can slip out of the country. That's going to be his best bet route."

"Let's just wait there and I'll intercept him," responded Rusty. "They'll probably send the Black Raven after him, once they discover the list is of no value to them. I believe he has a small flat about three blocks from the Embassy, so he'll probably go there to get his disguise together before fleeing Poland. As I recall, he's a master at disguising himself, isn't he?"

"Yes he is. What are you thinking?"

"Well, as much as I hate to terminate one of our own, it seems to be a necessity. He has already taken out one of ours, and would have been the cause of ten more being terminated, if you hadn't intervened so quickly. I want to try to get this taken care of before the Raven shows up. I would rather not come in contact with him right now; it would probably turn into one hell of a battle."

"Agreed," said Smokey.

Rusty was getting ready to leave, when the phone rang. Smokey answered it, "Hello. Yes, he's right here, hang on." He handed the phone to Rusty.

Taking the phone, Rusty said, "Hello, who's this?"

"Sundance? Ah'm glad ah caught ya. This is Jim Tahte. Look, ah know the two of you were fond of each othah when you met at one of my pahrties a few yeahrs back and I know you've seen each othah since. Ah'm sorry to have ta tell ya this, but ah thought ah'd bette' be the one. The Black Raven has killed Sonyah. He tohrtuhred her."

Rusty fell back into his chair in shock. "Thanks, Jim." He then gently set the phone back down on the desk, stayed sitting in the chair for a few moments, numb. Suddenly, he stood up, whirled around toward the door, and slammed his huge fist right through Smokey's office wall and into the secretary's office. He looked at Smokey and saw both fear and concern in his eye, but uttered not a word.

Opening the office door, Smokey checked on his secretary. Seeing she was just a little shaken, but otherwise was all right, he asked, "Could you please bring in two coffees, one with sugar and cream? Thank-you." He then landed her a note that said, "Make Sundance's special." Nodding acknowledgment, she headed into the break-room.

Smokey turned to Rusty who was emptying his pockets. "Sit!"

"I'm resigning. Here are my credentials, the weapons are mine."

"Fine, now that you've quit, are you going to sit down and explain yourself? You at least owe me that much." Smokey stood at the door, waiting for Rusty to comply. He could see the wheels churning in Rusty's brain as he sat down. He knew that whatever this was all about, there wasn't going to be a good side.

The secretary walked into the office as Smokey was taking his seat. She set the cups down in front of the men and excused herself as Smokey thanked her.

"Drink your coffee and let's talk about whatever it is Jim Tate called you about," Smokey said calmly. "You know I'll find out anyway, so you might as well tell me now."

Slowly Rusty started relating to Smokey all about the relationship he and Sonya had developed over the last six years and about the plans they had made. "And now she's dead," he stated. "The Raven has killed her and I don't know why."

Having lost his own wife to cancer three years ago, Smokey was able to relate to the pain Rusty was feeling. He began telling Rusty about her. Then he complimented Rusty on their discretion. "Jim and I had no clue about the depth of your relationship with Sonya. I doubt the Raven did either, so whatever his reasons, I'm sure it had nothing to do with you.

"Finish your coffee, we are going to put together a strategy for this whole mess. Of course, the Raven is yours, that's a promise. Just make sure you get your emotions under control, or he won't be the one going down. You will. I think we can use this current situation with the Wasp to draw him out for you."

Feeling calmer and a lot less shaky, Rusty put his coffee down. "So what's in the coffee?"

"Just a mild relaxant to calm your nerves. I needed you to be able to talk rationally, so we could work on a plan. Now Sundance, I can't say it enough, I don't want you to forget what I've drilled into you all these years. `You can't get emotional when you need to be at your best for an assignment. You'll lose your edge and get yourself killed.' I think this is the first time I've ever seen you lose your cool, in all the years I've known you. This is not the time to start."

Rusty apologized and tried to refocus on the prior conversation and get back down to business. "So where were we then? We know he will probably go back to the flat to change. . . ."

"Not now, Sundance," Smokey interrupted. "We can figure it all out later on the plane. I've given you the Raven; I don't think any other operative could handle him anyway. Right now I want you to go have a good dinner, eat as much as you can. Then I want you to get a good night's sleep. I have a sleeping aid that will get you through the night if you need it. Tomorrow morning we'll be on our way to Poland for the funeral."

Rusty looked at Smokey quizzically. "Are you going too?"

"Of course," Smokey said with a quiet reassuring smile. "I should be there for diplomacy reasons, and I want to be there for you. I'm not letting you go through this alone, friend. You're going to need to try to hold down your anger and grief until this is all settled. I'll be there to help you as much as I can. I know it's going to be rough, but I'm here for you."

Standing up, the two of them shared a big hug, "Thanks for everything, Smokey." Rusty started to leave the room.

"Aren't you forgetting something?" Smokey said.

Rusty gave him a half smile, and went back to pick up his credentials. Then he left to get something to eat. "I'll see you in the morning," he said, and then closed the door. Nodding to the secretary, he left the building.

Back in his room, Rusty got out his switchblade knife; it was an awesome weapon. He knew that was what the Raven would probably use. He was damn good with it. *But then, so am I.* His thoughts turned to Sonya. He had loved her so much, *What will I do with my life now that you're gone? The Raven has destroyed my life.* The desire for revenge consumed him so much, he could spit blood just thinking about it. He pictured slicing the Raven so deeply, that every time he moved he would think of Sundance and remember why he had come at him. *It's going to be one hell of a fight. Of course I'm really going to have to try to kill him, but a crippling injury would be satisfying. I'll have to try to keep my emotions out of it. That's going to be the toughest part of this whole thing. If I can't do that, I'll be handing The Raven an advantage, and I can't afford to do that. There are a hundred different things that might happen in this battle. I'll have to make sure I'm calm enough to notice every chance at an opening. Logic, instinct and talent will be the keys. What will happen, will happen.*

Sundance slid the weapon back into its sheath, and began musing on the whys of the situation. *Why did the Raven kill you, Sonya? It doesn't make any sense. You only did light weight intelligence for the Polish government. You didn't even carry a weapon! There is no way he found out about our relationship. Even Jim and Smokey were surprised about that one. Did you stumble onto something and he found out about it? But what? Whatever it was, it was important enough for them to try to torture you for it. I know you would never reveal any information enough for them to try to torture you for it. I know you would never reveal any information you had, even if it meant your death. It might be years before I find out why he killed you. You weren't deep enough into the intelligence game to be making regular reports to them, so I doubt even Jim or Smokey knows why. I probably won't get any information out of the Raven either. Sonya, I swear, no matter how long it takes, I will get to the bottom of this; but I have a feeling only time and patience will solve this riddle.*

Deciding he should turn in and get some rest, he turned out the light and crawled into bed. Falling asleep, he entered a world full of Sonya—her laughter, her walk, everything about her—what a waste of a beautiful, beautiful lady.

11

Smokey and Rusty boarded the plane to Poland the next morning. Smokey could tell that Rusty had lost his spark and enthusiasm. "I want you to take two of these pills to make you feel better. Then when we get to the Embassy, we're going to the gym for a hell of a workout. I want you to do this every day until you meet up with the Wasp and the Raven. It will help you get through the worst of it." He then handed Rusty a bottle of the pills. "I don't want you to take too many though. Follow the directions on the prescription bottle. If you take even one pill too many, it will be more harmful than helpful."

"Yes, Boss." Rusty didn't know what they were, but as long as they helped him get through this horrible feeling he had, he didn't care.

Soon they arrived in Poland, and Jim Tate greeted them in the terminal. He gave Rusty a big hug, "How're ya doin' Sundahnce? Ah'm so sohrry for what has hahppened."

"Thanks, I want to talk to you later about how it happened. I need as much information as you have."

"Ah'll shahre everythin' ah have and try to get more by then. Ah have some of my mahrines making inquiries," Jim told him.

Arriving at the Embassy, Jim elaborately motioned the two of them inside. "Welcome to mah humble home," he said.

Grinning, Smokey responded, "Humble home my butt."

Rusty chuckled for the first time since receiving the news about Sonya.

Jim took Smokey to his room, which, upon Smokey's discreet request, happened to be next to Rusty's. Rusty went into his own room to get changed for their workout. They then headed to

46

the gym for one of the hardest workouts they'd ever had. After a steaming hot shower, Rusty had to admit he felt a lot better than he had in awhile.

The funeral was held the following day. There were a lot of Sonya's friends and acquaintances there. Most of them Rusty did not know, since they had tried to keep their relationship quiet. When Rusty got to the open casket and saw her wearing the same blue dress she had been wearing the first night he had met her, the tears started flowing. He fell to his knees and leaned over to kiss her good-bye, "I love you sweetheart." Then he thought he heard her say, *I love you too.*

Smokey and Jim helped him to his feet and walked with him back to their seats. Smokey handed him two pills. Realizing he had forgotten to bring some himself, he took them and swallowed them quickly. "Thanks."

The ceremony was beautiful, and then they followed the casket to the gravesite. There was a Polish honor guard that did a gun salute, some American marines then did one as well, and then the American flag and the Polish flag that were both laid across the coffin, were removed, folded, and given to one of Sonya's relatives. Rusty guessed that she was probably the younger sister Sonya had told him was in America. She hadn't mentioned any other relatives to him. Medals of Honor were then presented to Sonya postmortem, one from the Polish government and one from the American government.

There was a wake planned for after the funeral, but Rusty couldn't handle any more pain that day, so Jim went to the host to make their excuses. The drive back to the Embassy was a quiet one, with each man lost in his own thoughts. When they arrived, Rusty excused himself and went up to his room.

"Ahre ya goin' to be ahlright?" Jim called up the stairs.

"I'll be okay. It's just been a tiring and emotional day."

12

The next morning, Rusty was up bright and early. He went down to the gym for another great workout. He found that working out did more for him than the pills and decided to stop taking them. It was time to get his house back in order (so to speak). He went to the dining room to meet Jim and Smokey for breakfast.

"Hey, Sundance, it's great to see you almost back to your old self!" Smokey exclaimed, when Rusty walked in the room. He knew things weren't back to normal yet, it would probably be a long haul, but at least he knew Sundance was working on getting there.

"Thanks for being there yesterday," Rusty said. "I'm indebted to you."

"We know you'd be there fohr us if the taybles were tuhrned. That's what friends ahre fohr, so don't go stahrt'n ta keep score now," said Jim.

"Exactly," agreed Smokey. "Now, have you decided how you are going to handle the Wasp and the Black Raven?"

"I've got some ideas," Rusty responded. "I think I'll go on up to my room and work on the details now, so if you'll excuse me." As he left the room, Smokey gave Jim a thumb's up signal. Jim nodded back.

Back in his room, Rusty started reading everything he could on both operatives. He knew he had a hell of a challenge ahead of him. Hopefully he would be able to take care of the Wasp before the Black Raven showed up; but whatever happened, he had to make sure he was able to dispense with both of them.

After studying everything he had on the two of them, he

picked up the phone and called Jim. "Hi Jim, can we get together? I need to go over what else you've managed to pick up about what happened to Sonya."

"Sure, meet me in the dinin' room. Ah was just about to have some lunch. Shall ah order somethin' for you?"

"No thanks, I'm too wound up to eat right now. See you in a few minutes."

Downstairs, Rusty walked into the dining room just as Jim finished ordering. "Hey there. So, have you been able to find anything else out about why Sonya was terminated? Have you heard anything about when the Wasp or the Raven might show up?"

"Whoa. Easy boy, one question at a time," Jim laughed. "Ah know you'hre anxious, and Ah'll tell you everythin' Ah've found out. To ahnswer yohr first question, it seems that Sonyah must have had some infohmation that the Rahyven wanted. The consensus is that he went too fah tryin' to get it out of her. We don't know what the inforhmation was, but it must'a been somethin' vera imporhtant foh him to step that fah out of bounds. Smokey is really worried 'bout that and is tryin' to find out what infohmation Sonyah might'a had.

"To ahnswer yohr second question, the Wasp will prob'ly show up heeh in the next couple of dahys, and if he's as pahranoid as he nohmally is, it'll prob'ly be layte at night, so as not to be seen. The Rayven will definitely be comin' after him, but we aren't sure how fah behind he is. Ya'll prob'ly have time to handle the Wasp before the Rahyven gets heeh, which is crucial, 'cause he still has the items Smokey gayve him to give to the aygent that was killed. He may try to use them as a bargainin' tool with the Rahyven. We need to avoid that."

Rusty knew exactly what the three items were—a microchip and two sets of papers that were extremely informative on the work various agents had been assigned to.

"When ya tayke care of the Wasp, try not to let it be known

49

foh a while," Jim continued, "ya don't want the Rahyven to get wind of it and head back home. If he finds out, ya may have to track him down and deal with him on his home tuhrf instead of heeh, and you don't want ta lose that advantage."

13

Now began the waiting game Rusty hated so much. He decided he would scope out the Wasp's flat for the best spot for the assassination. It needed to be done clean and simple. Not wanting Smokey to send in any back up to get in his way, Rusty avoided telling him or Jim where the flat was before leaving the Embassy. When he arrived, he pulled out the set of skeleton keys he had brought with him, and found one that would open the flat. Once inside, he started searching for anything that would connect the Wasp to the CIA. Gathering these items as well as any weapons he could find, and all the make-up and disguises, he sealed everything into plastic bags. He would give the bag to Jim tomorrow to send by courier to Smokey. Feeling that he had done what he could for now, he then headed back to the Embassy. Knowing he would probably have trouble sleeping, he took a sleeping pill and went to bed.

The next morning, he rolled out of bed, went to the gym for a good workout, showered and went down to join Jim for breakfast, bringing the package with him.

Taking the package, Jim said, "Ah'll make sure Smokey gets this ASAP. Are you ready for tomorra' night?"

"I have a few last minute things to do, but on the whole I'm ready for just about anything that might happen. Make sure your marines are looking for me on my way back in, I may need some assistance. Hopefully it won't come to that."

"Not a problem, Sundahnce," Jim assured him. "Ah'll take care of it. You just concentrayte on tomorra' night's excursion."

"For that I have to find some way to get Sonya out of my head," Rusty said. "I can't stop thinking about her and what the Raven did to her."

"Ah know it still hurts liyke hell," Jim said. "Try to concentrayte on all the good times ya had with her and cherish those mem'ries. The Rahyven can't tayke those away from you. After a while the good mem'ries will dominate and the pain will slowly fade."

"Thanks," Rusty said wearily, and then headed back up the stairs. Once he was in his room, he started checking his weapons. It was a meditative chore for him, and it didn't hurt to make sure everything was working properly, just in case he ran into the Raven earlier than anticipated. He was going to need every advantage he could muster, while trying to keep his emotions in check during the struggle, or it could very well end up being his last one.

When his weapons (and his mind) were all in order, he started going back over all the information he had on the two operatives. He needed to be prepared for anything. He had a gut feeling this would be his roughest assignment yet; not that he feared the Raven, but he did respect his talents and capabilities. He knew it wasn't going to be a walk in the park. He had to win this one for Sonya, without thinking about her while doing it. It was going to be difficult. He knew he was a little stressed out, but thought, *Nothing a good night's sleep and a hard workout can't take care of. Then I should be just fine.*

14

The next morning, after his workout, Rusty met Jim for their habitual morning breakfast.

"Everythin' seems to be right on schedule," Jim informed him. "The Wasp is just outside the city and seems to be waitin' foh nightfall; and the Raven isn't too far away eitheh. It could be close. Ya might want to get an eahrly stahrt, just in case things stahrt happenin' a little eahlier than anticipated. Betteh safe than sorry, I always say."

"Thanks for the info and the advice," Rusty said. "I'll keep that in mind."

"Well, ah wish you all the best, Sundahnce, and ah hope ya have a hell of a lot of good luck," Jim said adamantly.

Rusty grinned, "I'll need all I can get, and probably a little help from upstairs too."

"Ahmen to that."

Back in his room, the afternoon seemed to drag out forever; but being impatient wouldn't help a bit. Rusty checked his gas pellet pistol, making sure the poison dart chamber was full. Then he cleaned his switchblade and made sure it was sharper than a razor. When he finished with it, a falling piece of hair separated into two upon contact with the edge. He knew the rest of his weapons were in good shape, having checked them out last night. He felt his mind racing over everything that he wanted to keep straight about how he wanted it all to go down, but knew it was a useless exercise. In a struggle to the death, nothing went as you planned. All you could do was rely on your intelligence, wits, training and any other edge you might get during the struggle.

At seven o'clock, Sundance left the Embassy and drove

down to the spot he had picked out earlier. He would stay in the car for now, taking periodical walks to keep warm. He started in on the simple supper supplied by the Embassy kitchen. The two sandwiches were his favorite, rare roast beef on pumpernickel bread with lots of mustard. Relishing every bite, they were gone in no time.

Around midnight, Sundance got out of the car again and wondered if the Wasp was even coming, then about a quarter of a block from the flat, he saw movement. It was the Wasp. Looking around some more, he saw no sign of the Raven yet. Silently walking in the shadows to intercept the Wasp, he had his gas pistol out. The Wasp gasped when he saw him. "Sundance?"

"Why'd you turn traitor, Wasp?" Sundance asked.

"I needed the money. I was ready to retire, and my pension wasn't going to be enough."

Sundance shot him once in the neck with a dart and caught him as he fell. He was dead within ten seconds. Searching the Wasp's pockets, he took his weapons, found the items Smokey needed and took both his real and fake passports. Letting the Wasp drop to the ground, he walked over to pick up the briefcase.

"I'll take that."

Turning, Sundance saw the Raven approaching. With a cynical grin he said, "You'll have to come through me to get it." Taking a step backwards, he waited with knife poised to see what the Raven's next move would be.

The Raven had his knife out in a flash and the moment Sundance had been waiting for in anticipation and dread had finally arrived.

"Why did you go after Sonya?" asked Sundance, as he began closing the gap between himself and the Raven. "She wasn't a threat to you, or did she have something on you?"

Sensing that Sundance had asked the question for more than just professional reasons, the Raven declined to answer. They began circling each other looking for weaknesses.

"I'll kill you for what you did to her," Sundance snarled. Finding an opening, he darted in with his knife, scoring on Raven's neck. The Raven moved in also, scoring on Sundance's wrist. Neither wound was serious and they started grappling. Sundance grabbed the Raven's right wrist to immobilize his knife hand; the Raven did likewise to Sundance's left wrist, leaving Sundance's right hand free. Then they were scuffling with no holds barred, anything to get the upper edge.

Managing to switch his knife to his right hand, Sundance made a quick thrust for the Raven's jugular vein. Missing, he caught him in the left eye. Meanwhile, the Raven had gotten his knife into his left hand and made a deadly thrust to Sundance's heart, just missing it by an inch. The Raven was in such excruciating pain; he let go of Sundance, picked up the briefcase and ran towards his car. Knowing the Raven was too far for the poison dart gun, Sundance went for his 9mm and squeezed off three shots, all of which hit their target. One bullet hit the Raven's hand, forcing him to drop the briefcase. The other two hit his upper and mid back. The Raven slumped as the bullets hit, but he made it into his car and disappeared into the night. Badly wounded, Sundance managed to get the briefcase and got into his car and made for the Embassy. The marines on guard recognized his car as it careened toward them and began calling for help. Jim Tate heard the noise and came running from his room, wearing his robe and barking out orders. One marine went to get a doctor; two more helped him from his car and into the house. When they had removed his coat and got him settled on the couch, Sundance asked everyone except Jim to leave the room for a moment. "Can you get me one of those courier bags?" Sundance then pulled out all the items he had taken from The Wasp, put them into the bag with the briefcase and sealed it. "The Wasp is terminated, but the Raven showed up immediately after. He is seriously wounded, has lost his left eye and will have a huge scar on the left side of his face. He also took three bullets as he was getting into his car, but he managed to get away."

"Ah'll make sure Smokey gets all the details tonight when ah talk to him," said Jim, "and these ihtems'll go with the courier pouch tomorra'."

The doctor had arrived by now, and started removing Sundance's clothes. "Jim, can you put my weapons up here near my head?" he asked. "And if anything happens to me, I want them to be buried with me." Jim promised and left him to the doctor's administrations. Sundance then passed out.

Jim went to his office to put the bag for Smokey into the courier pouch marked "Top Secret—For Smokey's Eyes Only." He then called one of the marines in to take the Wasp's suit, conceal it in a garbage bag, and take it to a dumpster across town. He then went back to the makeshift operating room.

Sundance was set up with an IV of plasma, to replace what he had lost, and the doctor had just finished sewing him up. "It's all in the hands of the Maker now," he said. "Here are some antibiotics and pain killers for when he wakes up. Make sure he gets lots of rest."

"Thanks, Doc." Jim then walked the doctor to the door. 'Ah'll call ya if anythin' changes." Then he went back to the room to sit with Sundance, and called Smokey.

"I'm sorry, but he is sleeping right now," the voice at the other end said. "Can you call back in about four hours?"

"Ah don't give a damn if he's sleeping," Jim roared. "Go wayke him up and tell 'im it's Jim Tahyte."

In a few minutes, Smokey came on the line. Jim told him everything that had gone down. After listening to Jim, Smokey said, "I'm sending you an air-evac plane as soon as I can line one up. Get him in an ambulance and to the airport to be there when it arrives. I want to get him the best care possible for those wounds. There is a very fine hospital and staff here on the CIA grounds."

Jim told him about Sundance's request, "Well, hopefully it won't come to that," Smokey replied, "but we will certainly honor any requests he's made."

Smokey then called Judge Hardaway to tell him that Rusty was in critical shape due to a run in with a foreign operative. "I'll let you know as soon as he's settled in. I've taken care of the plane arrangements for you and your daughter."

The air-evac plane landed the next morning. The ambulance was already there waiting. Smokey picked up the courier pouches and said, "Thanks for everything, Jim. I'll keep you posted on his progress. I'll send a couple of agents to clear out the rest of the Wasp's possessions at the flat. Try and find out anything you can about how the Raven is faring."

"Ah'll take care of all that, you take care of him."

Once Rusty was loaded on the plane, they took off, heading back to the U.S. There were two doctors aboard to work on him. As they checked him out one of them commented, "If it wasn't for this massive chest of his, he probably wouldn't be here."

Part IV

Recovering

15

It was two weeks later when Rusty finally awoke from the coma he had slipped into. When he opened his eyes, he saw the judge and Barbara sitting on either side of his bed. Both of them were busy reading books and didn't notice he was awake right away.

In his fifties, Judge Hardaway, a tall lean and extremely intelligent man, was still in excellent shape and considered quite handsome, with brown hair graying at the temples. His deep-set brown eyes reminded one not to mess around in his courtroom. With the same brown hair and deep-set brown eyes, Barbara was obviously her father's daughter. *Motherhood seems to have matured her. She doesn't look as carefree as the last time I saw her. What the hell are they doing here in Poland?*

Squeezing Barbara's hand, he verbalized his thought, "Hey kiddo, you guys didn't have to come all the way to Poland. I'd have been in the States soon."

Startled, Barbara almost dropped her book. Then, happy to see he had come around, she grinned at him. "Well gee, the last time I looked out that window over there, I would have sworn I was in Washington, D.C. at the CIA headquarters with you," she drawled.

Looking sheepish, he turned to the Judge. "I guess I blew that one, huh."

"Don't worry about it son. You did great. It's good to hear your voice again," the judge responded, his sense of relief evident in his voice. "You may not believe it listening to her, but you had us all worried." Seeing the unasked question in Rusty's eyes, he continued, "It's been two weeks since they evacuated you from Poland."

Feeling a sense of loss, followed by a surge of strength and determination go through him, Rusty became all business. "Well then, I have certainly laid around here long enough then, haven't I?" Removing the IV from his arm, he continued. "Can someone get me a pen and some paper?"

After scribbling a list of items he wanted he turned to his foster sister. "Babs, can you do me a big favor? Can you run down to the Base Exchange and pick these things up for me? Thanks."

Taking the list from him, she got up to leave. "You know I hate it when you call me that," she growled as she left the room.

Once she was out of the room Rusty started removing the catheter, grimacing from the burning sensation.

"What do you think you're doing?" asked the Judge.

"I'm getting rid of this damn thing. It's time to rejoin the living."

Once it was out, the Judge helped him to the bathroom and went back out to the room. After painfully relieving himself, Rusty looked around and noticed there was a shower with both shampoo and soap supplied. Sticking his head out the door, he called out, "Can you get me a couple of towels? I'm going to take a hot shower."

He spent the next few minutes just letting the hot water beat down on him, soothing out all the aches and pains he was feeling. Twenty minutes later, he finally turned off the shower feeling energized and ready to take on the world. Just then a nurse walked into the bathroom.

"What do you think you're doing?" she exclaimed.

"Well, from the looks of things, I'd say I've just had one hell of a nice shower." He then opened the shower door, grabbed one of the towels, put it around his waist, stepped from the shower, grabbed the other towel and began drying himself off.

"Do you normally do that when women are present?" asked the nurse indignantly.

"Only if they are silly enough to stand there and watch," he bantered back. "I'm sure I don't have anything you haven't seen before."

The nurse turned beet-red. Rusty thought she looked to be young, maybe in her mid-twenties. Barbara knocked on the door before entering. Looking at the nurse wondering why she was blushing so much, she handed Rusty the things he had requested. Motioning the nurse ahead of her, she left him to finish up. After shaving, brushing his teeth and combing out his hair, he felt like a million bucks. He re-entered the room, headed back to his bed, and asked the nurse for a clean set of clothes.

"I'll bring you some pajamas. No matter what you may want to believe, you are not ready to leave this hospital just yet," she informed him authoritatively. He grinned and waved her out.

"Boy, you sure look and smell a whole lot better," Barbara exclaimed.

"Thanks, I feel it."

The nurse came back in with some clean pajamas. Two doctors were following right on her heels. "Did it take all three of you to carry one pair of pajamas?" he asked cockily.

"Well, it looks like you feel a lot better today," said the doctor closest to Rusty.

"Now that I've gotten rid of all those damned tubes and had a decent shower, I certainly do."

The doctor started a quick examination, listening to his heart and checking his blood pressure. Then he asked Rusty to move his arm up and down, normally. When he did, Rusty realized he only had about half his normal range of motion. "What the hell is that about?" he asked.

"You had a knife wound that caused some damage to the nerves and tendons in the area. It could be a couple of years before you regain full range of motion, if you ever do. Judging by your miraculous recovery so far, I wouldn't be at all surprised if you got it all back a lot sooner than that, though."

"So, when do I get to leave this place?" Rusty asked.

"Maybe tomorrow morning. We need to run some tests first. I'll set them up for this afternoon. Go ahead and get dressed—in the pajamas, that is." The doctor smiled at him and said, "And stop giving the nurses such a hard time."

While Rusty was in the bathroom dressing, the doctor left the room and Smokey entered. Seeing him, the Judge got up.

"Come on Barbara, let's leave these guys alone and go get something to eat. We'll see you later, Rusty." Nodding to Smokey, he continued, "Thanks for all the hospitality. We really appreciate all the good care you're giving this boy of mine."

"It's the least we can do," Smokey replied, smiling.

Rusty came back into the room as they left. Smokey pulled a chair up to the head of Rusty's bed.

"We've got to talk."

"It's my arm, isn't it," Rusty said with a grimace.

"I'm afraid so. We have to put you into semi-retirement for now; but we still need to have your expertise available to us on occasion. Although it goes against my better judgment, you still get first crack at The Raven, so don't worry about someone else taking him out. You've earned the right. I really appreciate you taking care of that whole situation with The Wasp and retrieving all the stuff he had."

"Goes with the territory," Rusty grumbled, still dealing with the forced retirement.

Smokey continued as if Rusty hadn't said anything. "The doctor says you will probably get full range of motion within a couple of years, if you work at rehab real hard. With your record, I wouldn't be at all surprised if it was more like a year and a half, or even sooner. We can talk again when the time arrives. I still want you to be careful though. Keep your weapons with you at all times—Garth too. You both still have plenty of enemies.

"By the way," Smokey finished up, "The Raven has lost his left eye and his right shoulder doesn't work very well, thanks to one of the slugs you put into him. So if you do happen to meet up with him before you're one hundred percent, it could still be a close to even match."

"Thanks for the info. I'm kind of tired now. Can we continue this in the morning?"

"Not a problem, I'm done for now anyway. You get some rest." With that, Smokey left the room, closing the door behind him softly.

16

The next morning, the Judge and Barbara were heading home. Rusty was ready to leave as well. He wanted to get to the ranch as soon as possible. Smokey brought Rusty some of his clothes, as well as his weapons. While getting dressed, he noticed that the switchblade was new. It felt and looked great. Better than the last one he'd had.

"It's a new steel we've been working on. They're calling it ATS34. It's stronger than the steel we've used for knives in the past," Smokey explained.

"Thanks for everything, Smokey," he said, putting the knife in his back pocket. "I'll stay in touch."

"Keep that secure line in place so I can reach you if I need to," Smokey told him. "You're one of the best operatives I've ever had."

"Thanks. I'll just be a phone call away if you need me."

"Do you still have cottages available at that ranch of yours?"

"I sure do, you're welcome there any time."

"No thanks, maybe in a couple of years, " Smokey said. "Actually, I had someone else in mind. Do you remember Jake Gunner?"

"The Cowboy? Yeah, I remember him, why?"

"Well, he's coming out of rehab sometime in late April and could really use a quiet place to recuperate for a couple of years."

"What the hell happened to him?" Rusty asked.

"He was ambushed over in Vietnam, and by the time he could get help, gangrene had set in. He lost his foot. He has a prosthetic one now, and should soon be walking, or even running, without many problems. He's fairly depressed though, as you can imagine;

but between you and Garth, it shouldn't take too much to get him back on track. He could probably help you out, he's one hell of a carpenter."

"Send him over, when he's ready. I have some plans for the ranch that can use a good carpenter. Besides, it seems to be turning into a great place for injured and retired operatives."

17

Rusty reached the ranch in late January. Coming up the drive he saw Garth and Sandy rushing out of the house to greet him. They walked him up to the house, Sandy fussing over him the whole way.

"Stop being such a mother hen, Sandy," Garth laughingly told her. "Give the man space to breathe. He looks fine; he just needs some intense physical therapy and lots of fresh mountain air. He'll be as good as new in no time."

Rusty laughed with him, grabbed Sandy and gave her a big, strong hug. "See, not as much a weakling as you thought."

Flustered, Sandy huffed and went into the house ahead of them.

Dinner was ready within about fifteen minutes, and over the meal, Rusty filled them in on what had happened to Sonya. After dinner, Garth and Sandy went off to bed, leaving Rusty brooding in front of the fireplace.

Things began to settle into a steady rhythm with Garth and Rusty taking care of things on the ranch and Sandy taking care of the house. Spring began showing signs of an early arrival, bringing fresh life to the ranch.

In late March, Garth received a call that his father was very ill. As they were getting ready to leave the ranch, he said, "We'll probably only be gone about a month. Is that alright?"

"Take as long as you need to. For goodness sakes, you don't need my permission. This is your home too, and always will be! You can come and go as you please. Give your father my best and stay as long as you need to."

Thanking him, Sandy gave him a big hug and planted a kiss

on his cheek. "We'll be back as soon as we can. I've put together some meals for you to warm up. They're in the freezer. Take care of yourself and don't get into any trouble."

Rusty watched until they were out of sight, then he turned and entered the house to start the day's chores.

Part V

Back at the Ranch

18

April had arrived, and Rusty was heading back to the Ranch with his truck full of supplies. He liked to be well stocked and had just spend the day shopping for the next two months.

It was a little cold out, considering the time of year, but the air was invigorating and the fog was dissipating. *What a gorgeous, peaceful day this is,* he thought to himself as he started heading up the private road that led to the ranch. Suddenly he saw movement on the hill to his right. Stopping the truck, he reached for his binoculars. *Who the hell could that be?* Then he spotted two little girls, who were obviously identical twins. They were both dressed in thin cotton dresses, knee socks and tennis shoes with nothing but windbreakers for warmth. *They must be freezing up there.*

Rusty put the binoculars back into the truck and headed up the hill. He was about ten feet from them when suddenly they stepped out from behind a boulder. They were holding rocks in their hands.

"Don't come no closer," the nearest one called out; "or we'll throw these big rocks at you."

Rusty sat down where he was. "I certainly wouldn't want you to hurt me with those big rocks. What if I just sit down here and we can talk?" Rusty took out his FBI badge and tossed it up to the girls. It landed in the grass in front of them. "Take a look at my badge," he told them, hoping to gain their trust. They looked really scared.

One of the twins picked the badge up and showed it to her sister. Then she asked Rusty, "What does FBI mean?"

Looking for a simple way of explaining it to them, he asked, "Well, you know what a policeman is, right?"

"Yeah."

"Well," Rusty said, "Most policeman are policeman for a certain city or town. I am a policeman for the whole United States."

"You're a policeman?" the closest twin asked incredulously.

Grinning, Rusty responded, "Yes I am. You don't have to worry about anything. I won't let anything hurt you now. It's my job to help people that are in trouble or who are lost and need help.

The twins whispered together for a minute, and the closest twin asked him, "Where's your special police clothes?"

"Do you mean my uniform?"

"Policemen always wear special police clothes."

"Not all policemen wear uniforms, especially policemen that go after really bad men. We wouldn't want them to know we're policemen until it's time for us to arrest them and take them to jail."

Apparently coming to a decision, the other twin stepped forward. "Do you have any food?"

"Why yes I do," Rusty said cheerfully. "I have all kinds of food down in my truck. I've got the heater on, so the cab is nice and warm too. Do you want to go down there with me and we can talk there?"

After more whispering, they agreed. Dropping their rocks, they walked over to Rusty. Holding out a hand to each of them, he led them down the hill to the truck. *They both seem to be a little warm. They must be getting a fever.* Once inside, he got them bundled up.

"I have a great ranch not too far from here. You can have warm baths and hot food there if you want to. Then we can figure out what's going on and what we should do with you. Okay?"

"Okay."

Going to the back of the truck and opening up the camper, he dug out two 7-Ups and some potato chips. Getting into the driver's seat, he opened the sodas and chips and handed them to the twins. "Slowly now. You don't want to get sick."

"Thanks, Mister."

"You're welcome. My name is Rusty, what are your names?"

The one nearest him said, "I'm Stacy. My sister is Tracy. We're almost five and a half years old." Then she started drinking her soda and eating chips.

Tracy just looked at him solemnly with her big green eyes that were almost too big for her face. Rusty started the truck and headed for the ranch.

19

Once they arrived, he carried them up to the house and into the bathroom. Looking around, he found some of Sandy's bubble bath beads and started a bath for the girls.

"Okay, in you go. First a bath, then some lunch. Here is soap and a couple of washcloths, wash up and then call me when you're ready for your hair to be washed. I'll leave the door open so I can hear you."

He went into the kitchen and started heating up some tomato soup and made a couple of peanut butter and jelly sandwiches for them. Then he started thinking about what they could wear. The clothes they had arrived in were filthy and would need to be washed before they could be worn again. Then he remembered that Barbara had a bunch of kids' clothes that he was supposed to have taken to the Salvation Army, but hadn't gotten around to yet. Finding them in the garage, he began digging through them. He was able to find some clean pants and t-shirts that would probably fit. They looked a little big, but that would make sleeping more comfortable, as they would have to double as pajamas for now. Shoes would have to wait, but he did find some cozy looking socks that would serve as slippers.

A small voice traveled up the hall to him, "Mister Rusty? We're ready."

Going back into the bathroom, he saw two giggling bubble girls. They had made beards and wigs from the bubbles. He laughed with them and went over to wash their hair. Once that was done and he'd rinsed them all off with the shower hose. He handed them each fluffy towels to dry with and then helped them get into the clothes he had found.

"But, Mister Rusty! These are boys' clothes," one of the girls said.

"Yeah, we're not boys," the other agreed.

"It's okay for girls to wear boys' clothes sometimes. Especially when they need something warm to wear," Rusty assured them.

"Oh," they both said uncertainly.

Then he helped them wrap their hair into smaller towels, like he used to do for his sister when they were growing up.

When they were ready, he led them over to the table where sandwiches and soup were waiting for them, then leaving them to eat he went back to the bathroom to get their clothes and put them in the washer. He then joined the girls at the table.

They seemed much more relaxed now that they were warm and had something to eat. He turned his operative eyes onto them. *To the untrained eye, it is probably hard to tell the difference between them. Tracy is left-handed and Stacy is right-handed. Tracy has a little birthmark on her right temple. She is the shy one. Stacy seems to be the one to take control when possible. They've got beautiful auburn hair to go with those big green eyes. They're going to be knockouts when they grow up—if they grow up. I wonder what's happened to them. Why were they alone on that hill? I'll have to see if I can backtrack their trail when I get a chance.*

After the girls had finished their lunch, he led them into the living room, where he had a fire going. He had Tracy sit on a stool in front of his chair and started combing out her hair. "So, tell me about your adventures. Do you know where home is?" he said. "I want to hear all about it."

"Well," Tracy started off solemnly. "A man came to our house and said daddy was hurt really bad."

"He said he was goin' to take us and Mommy to the hospital," Stacy added eagerly.

Tracy glared at her sister a moment and continued. "Stacy and me didn't like him and didn't want to go. We told Mommy, but she made us put our coats on. She gave us some lifesavers, cookies and juice to put in our pockets for later. When we were in the car, Mommy aks'd the man why he was goin' the wrong way. He didn't say nuthin'.''

Stacy interrupted her sister again, "He was a bad man. He said he and some other men had kilt our daddy. He said it was an accident. But he got a shot or somethin'. The man said it didn't work with Daddy's heart medicine. He said he wanted my daddy's formal."

Tracy took over the story again, "Mommy aks'd him what he was goin' to do now and he said he was goin' to kill us 'cause Mommy knew who he was. Then he hit her with his gun and she didn't move anymore. We were really scar't. Then the man went outside to go pee and we sneaked out of the car and ran away."

"Yeah," Stacy interrupted again, "we ran and ran as fast as we could and then hid in some bushes. We saw the man get back in the car. He didn't look in the back and didn't know we were gone. Then he left. We started runnin' again. We didn't know where to go. We were really scar't."

Tracy continued, "When it was night time, we found an old car; we ate our cookies and juice and went to sleep in the car. The next day we walked and walked and walked but we didn't see a road. We ate our lifesavers, but we were really hungry. Then we found a cave and went to sleep. We kept hearin' all kinds of animals, it was scary. The next mornin' we started walkin' again, then we saw you."

"Well you're safe now," Rusty assured them. "You are two very brave little girls and I'm really proud of you. You know, when I was a little boy, my mommy and daddy were killed by some bad men too; but everything has turned out all right for me, and it will for you too. Now, you two must be really tired; time for some sleep in a real bed. How's that sound?"

"Ahhhhh," they both said. "Do we have too?"

"Come on now," he said, and he carried them both into the

guestroom next to his room and tucked them in. They were both feeling a little feverish. *I hope that's just from the excitement and they aren't coming down with something.* "Sweet dreams, and don't worry about a thing. I'll take care of you from now on. Good night."

"Night, night."

20

After putting the clothes in the dryer, Rusty called the Judge. After telling him about everything that had happened, he said, "You know the parents are probably both dead. I'll have some inquiries made just to be sure though. In the meantime, draw up some legal documents making me sole guardian of them. If their parents really are dead, I want full custody. Be discreet though, I don't want the wrong people finding out they're here. In fact, if you can, backdate the guardianship paperwork about three years. It could save their lives if they can't be connected to their father. If you need any funds to make it happen, let me know."

"I'll take care of it," the Judge said.

"Thanks. I'll either be here or at the hospital if you need me. They both felt a little warm as I was putting them to bed. If they don't feel a little cooler soon, I'll take them in to emergency."

"Get a hold of Dr. Brown. He's a damn good doctor and is very discreet."

"I'll do that."

"I may need you or Babs to watch them for me for a couple of hours tomorrow. I want to see if I can backtrack their trail. There might be some clues at the spot where they left the car."

"Not a problem. Give either of us a call when you're ready."

Then Rusty called Smokey. "Can you see if you can find out anything about this matter? Is this something any of our operatives might be working on? If possible I need to verify that the parents are both dead, and if not, where they are."

"I'll see what I can find out for you," Smokey told him. "By the way, Jake Gunner is just about ready to head out to your place. He should be there around the twentieth."

"Great, Garth and Sandy aren't back yet, so I can really use the help."

"Jake is really looking forward to seeing you and Garth again."

"Thanks for your help, let me know what you find out."

"Well, if you need anything else, don't hesitate to call. We'll assist you in any way we can."

After hanging up the phone, Rusty went to get the clothes he had washed for the girls out of the dryer. While folding them, he reflected on the day, and on how fast he had become attached to the twins. He felt like a mother hen, what with the way he was worrying about them.

Later he sat down to watch the 6:00 news, but in the back of his brain, he was still fretting about the twins. He checked on them again at 7:00. Their fevers seemed to have risen, so he called Dr. Brown and asked him to meet them at the hospital. He went out and started the truck warming up. Grabbing a couple of extra blankets from the linen closet on his way to their room, he bundled them both up and carried them out to the truck.

As he was flying down Hwy 20 toward town, a siren started up behind him. He checked the rear view mirror and saw the lights flashing behind him. Not wanting to be delayed in getting the girls to the hospital, he ignored the CHP officers behind him and sped up even more, outdistancing them. He roared into town and was on two tires as he negotiated the turn to the hospital. As he pulled up at Emergency, he saw Dr. Brown and Geri waiting for them.

Seeing his questioning look as he got out of the truck, Geri said, "I just happened to be visiting Doc when you called."

Nodding, Rusty was busy extracting the girls from their seat belts when three CHP cars pulled in with sirens blaring. He glanced at them as he was pulling the girls out of the truck. "Geri, could you please park my truck while I get the girls inside?"

Geri glanced with raised eyebrows toward the CHPs that had pulled in, she replied, "Sure thing, Rusty."

"Thanks." Continuing to ignore the officers, he ran into Emergency carrying the girls. Medics met him at the door and helped him put the twins into wheel chairs. Rusty asked one of the medics, "Are any of the wings empty?" He didn't want anyone having access to the girls that wasn't authorized by him personally.

"The second floor has just been added, so it isn't really in full use yet," answered the medic closest to him. "I think the east wing may still be empty up there."

"Let's go!" They hurriedly wheeled the girls over to the elevator with Dr. Brown; the CHP officers were trailing behind them. It would probably have been an amusing sight, if it hadn't been so critical. As they got off the elevator, the head nurse came up to them demanding to know what was going on.

"I'm taking over this wing," Rusty told her.

"No you're not," she responded. "This is a public hospital, and I won't tolerate any shenanigans."

Rusty looked her square in the eye. "I'll tell you again, try to understand it this time. This wing is now mine. If you don't like it, you can get the hell out of here." Dr. Brown and the medics were coming around the corner with the girls. Both of the girls had IVs hooked up to their little arms. Rusty pointed to the nearest room. "Take them in there."

After the twins had settled in, and were resting a little easier, Rusty went over to the CHP officer. Geri had joined them by now and was standing with them. She grinned at him, "That was quite a little parade you were leading there. What's going on?"

"I've got two very sick little girls on my hands. I didn't have time to fool around explaining myself."

Dr. Brown approached the group. "If you'd brought them in any later, they might not have made it. They're both in grave condition and appear to have pneumonia. I've sent samples down to the lab to verify it. I've given them some medication to combat it, and we may have to put them into an alcohol-ice bath if the fevers don't come down."

The head nurse was carrying on with the medics and officers. "Get this man off my ward now."

"Excuse me," Rusty said as he showed her his FBI badge, "I'll say it one more time, this is my ward and you can leave it right now. As long as these girls are here, I don't want to see you up here again." The nurse left the room, slamming the door behind her.

"I think you just made an enemy," Dr. Brown told him.

"Do you think I care, at this point? How long do you think before the medication you've given them kicks in?"

"Well, to be honest with you, we'll just have to wait and see; but if this doesn't work, there is something else I can try. The girls are in pretty bad shape."

One of the CHP officers finally interrupted. "Excuse me sir, but we have to give you a speeding ticket and a ticket for reckless driving."

"Go ahead, I'll have it thrown out in the morning." Rusty showed him his FBI badge.

"Oh, to hell with it," the officer said. "Good luck with your daughters. Come on, boys, this is a waste of time." The CHP turned to leave.

Spotting Geri in the group, Rusty stopped her. "I think I might be able to fix you up with a guy you'd find real interesting." He then proceeded to regale Geri with all the qualities and tribulations of Jake Gunner.

She smiled. "I think I'd like to meet this gent," she said. "He could probably use some cheering up. What are you running up there anyway? A halfway house for disabled officers?"

Rusty laughed. "Could be. It certainly seems that way, doesn't it."

Dr. Brown came up to them and said; "All we can do for now is wait. If anything goes the least bit wrong, I've left instructions for the staff to call me at home. I think I'll go get some shut-eye, I suggest you do the same. Can I run you home, Geri?"

"Thanks," she said. "That would be nice. Good night, Rusty; we'll see you in the morning."

"Thanks for your help. I think I'll stay here. Good night."

21

Rusty went back to check on the twins. Their fevers were still high, but at least they appeared to be sleeping more peacefully. Reaching over, he kissed each one on the forehead.

One of the nurses came in, after checking the girls, she said, "They'll probably sleep through the night. You should get a good night's sleep and come back in the morning."

"I'm not leaving the hospital until the girls get through this," he told her. "If I get tired, I'll either find a chair to crash in, or I'll use a bed in the next room. I think I'll go get cleaned up though, if you could stay with them for a few minutes."

"Of course I can," the nurse said, smiling.

Rusty walked down the hall in search of a restroom. After cleaning himself up, he examined his reflection in the mirror. He could see the toll this crisis had taken on him already. He had only known these twins for less than a day, and he couldn't believe how close he had begun to feel to them. He felt as if he had known them all their lives. He couldn't fathom it; it just didn't make any sense.

As he was walking back to the room, he passed one of the executive offices. Looking in the window, he noticed a large leather chair that looked like it would recline like a Lazy-Boy. He tried the door, but it was locked. Reaching into his pocket, he pulled out a small tool and opened the lock with it. He grabbed the chair, and carried it over his head to the girl's room, and placed it between thee two girls' beds. After sitting down in it, and reclining halfway, he soon fell into a restless sleep.

It was six in the morning when Rusty woke up, and as the nurse had predicted, the twins were still sleeping. Feeling their foreheads, he found that they were still burning with fever. Going to the nurses' station, he poured himself a cup of coffee they had brewed. "How is everything progressing for the girls?" he asked the nurse on duty.

"There has been no change since last night," she answered. "Their fevers are both still 103 degrees. Breakfast will be served shortly, would you like me to order one for you?"

"Yes, please, I would appreciate that very much."

The morning passed very slowly. Around 10:00 A.M., two local policemen arrived. "Mr. Rusty Kincaid?"

"Yes, may I help you."

"I'm afraid you'll need to come with us; we're placing you under arrest."

"For what?"

"We've had a complaint from the head nurse. She has filed a complaint against you for assault. She claims you came in last night and took over the ward, threatening her in order to force her to leave her station and not come back."

"First of all, I'm a federal officer assigned to the protection of these two girls, and you won't be taking me anywhere. Second of all, she was obstructing me in carrying out my duty, so I dismissed her, and she may not return until these girls are well enough to leave this hospital. . . . I wouldn't do that if I were you," he told the younger of the two officers, who had started to pull out his revolver. "I don't think you want to die quite so young, Do you?" His own gun had appeared as if by magic and the young officer replaced his revolver in his holster.

"Do you have some type of credentials to verify your claims?" the older officer asked.

Rusty handed him the FBI badge and federal identification. After checking it out, the officer handed it back to him. "Everything seems to be in order."

"If you have any other questions, you can call the Agency in Washington, D.C.," Rusty told them. "Now if you don't mind the doctor has arrived and I'm sure he'd like to examine the girls." He motioned to Dr. Brown, who was standing in the doorway watching the scene. "Come on in Doc." The two officers left the room.

"What's going on?" Dr. Brown asked, as he walked in the room and started examining the twins.

"Oh the nurse from last night decided to cause some additional problems. I've handled it. How are the girls doing?"

"Well, I'm having a problem getting these fevers to break. I'm going to have to try a stronger antibiotic. You look like hell, didn't you get any sleep last night?"

Nodding toward the chair he had confiscated, he said, "I grabbed a little shut eye in that."

Doc shook his head in disapproval. "You need to get some real rest, or you aren't going to be of much use to them, when they start to recuperate. Why don't you at least go outside and get some fresh air. I'll stay with them a while."

Rusty agreed and went outside to find a phone booth. Finding one out on the plaza, he called the Judge. "How are you coming on those birth certificates and custody papers?"

"I got everything approved, with some help from Barbara and your pal Smokey. As soon as I receive them, I'll bring them over to you myself."

After thanking him and hanging up the phone, Rusty went over to the newsstand and bought a newspaper. He was on his way back to the room the girls were in, when he heard a hell of a racket going on down the hall. Going to see what was going on, he saw a tall, gray-haired gentleman yelling at one of the nurses. "Where the hell is my chair? Someone had better find it soon or there will be hell to pay!"

Rusty walked over to them. "Excuse me, but I appropriated it last night. I'm using it in Room 203 right now. So if you could find a different chair to use for a while, I would appreciate it."

"Who the hell do you think you are?" the man yelled, turning his ire onto Rusty.

As Rusty reached for his badge, the man was able to see his

weapons, and started backing up a little. Upon seeing the FBI badge, he blustered, "That still doesn't give you the right to break into my office and take my chair."

"I'm sorry you feel that way, since I will be continuing to use it until those girls get better."

The man threw his hands up in disgust and went back into his office. One of the nurses laughed. "You sure have shaken things up around here."

Rusty smiled. "I'm good at that." Then he walked back down the hall to see how the girls were doing.

"They're still sleeping," Doc told him. "I'll be back later to check on them."

Rusty settled back into the chair and fell asleep for another three hours, until a nurse walked in to give the twins some medicine. "How are they doing?"

"Not too good, right now; but Dr. Brown is a very good doctor. If anyone can bring them around, he can." The nurse smiled encouragingly at him and left the room.

Rusty started reading the paper he had purchased earlier, to pass the time.

Around seven P.M., Dr. Brown walked in. After checking them again, he turned to Rusty. "It doesn't look good. If things don't improve quickly, they may not make it through the night. I don't know what else I can do to help them." Rusty was stunned.

Dr. Brown left him with his thoughts and the girls, and ran into the Judge and Barbara coming down the hall. He told them what was going on, and warned them that if the twins did die, Rusty is going to need all the care and love they could give him.

In the room, Rusty was on his knees, holding both of the little fevered bodies tightly. He was praying as tears streamed down his cheeks. He could tell they had slipped into a coma, and his heart was breaking. *I can take out the best foreign agents and rescue those that need it from the most impossible situations, but all my strength and expertise can't help these two little girls. I already*

88

feel like they're my own. Taking care of these two little tykes would give me a new reason to live. I don't think I can handle losing them so soon after losing Sonya. "Please, Lord, please save these two little ones. Their lives have just begun. I'll do anything you require if you answer my prayer."

Rusty felt a warm glow and heard a voice say, *Open your eyes, Sundance. You have nothing to fear.* Rusty held the girls even tighter; afraid the voice would take them away from him. Then he heard the voice again. *Sundance; open your eyes. You have nothing to fear.* Opening his eyes, he saw an image of a beautiful angel dressed in a beautiful white flowing gown. She was spectacular. She had gold-flaxen hair, and her eyes were an intense deep blue. He could feel an immense amount of love flowing from her body. He tried to read her eyes but couldn't. She spoke again. *I am their Guardian Angel and I told them I would take them to a wonderful place to play with children like themselves. Then I heard your prayer. Do you, Sundance, solemnly promise to love them, protect them, and be their father until they become of age?*

"I promise to love them, protect them and to be their father until the day I take my last breath," Rusty swore.

Listen to me, Sundance. Your path will be very rocky and rough, so you will have to protect them with all the strength and knowledge you possess. All of your skills will be required, do not let your guard down, even once. Then she disappeared. Wondering if he had hallucinated the whole thing, Rusty held his two newly acquired daughters tightly against him.

Their fevers were still high. Suddenly, he felt drenched. Both girls were sweating buckets and all three of them were soaked. The fever had broken. Tracy opened her eyes. "Did you see our angel?"

"I sure did," he happily told her.

"She was going to take us to a place to play, but she said you wanted us to stay, and she told us you're going to be our new Daddy. That you'll protect us, so she sent us back."

"Wasn't she pretty?" Stacy asked him.

"She was the most beautiful lady I have ever seen," he told her solemnly. Then he started laughing and hugging them, with tears streaming down his face.

Barbara and the Judge rushed into the room just then to see what the ruckus was about. "What was that light coming out of here a minute ago?" Barbara asked. "We felt like we were moving in slow motion, coming down the hall."

"Well, this is going to be hard to believe, but the twins have a Guardian Angel, and she was visiting." Then he told them about the encounter.

"Well, I believe you," the Judge said. "There isn't any better explanation for what happened to us out there that I can think of. That was a really strange experience."

"How come she called you Sundance, instead of Rusty?" Stacy said.

"Well, at work, my name is Sundance; and I'm going to need all the skills and expertise that I have learned as Sundance to protect you girls."

"Oh." Both girls looked at him curiously, but he wouldn't say anything more about it.

"Barbara, could you go to the nurses' station and see if we can get some apple juice for the girls?" Rusty asked. "Also let them know that the girls need baths and clean pajamas, since their fevers have broken and to advise Dr. Brown of the situation. Thanks."

Dr. Brown arrived before the apple juice did. He couldn't believe what he saw. Both girls were wide-awake in Rusty's arms. "Do you think you can possibly let go of them long enough for me to examine them?" he asked.

Rusty complied with a grin. "I'll try, but it's a little difficult, Doc."

"I'm sure it is." Dr. Brown checked them over thoroughly and said, "If they are in as good of shape as they appear, I believe they will be able to go home tomorrow morning, but I want to keep them here overnight for observation. We certainly don't want them to have a relapse."

Barbara and the Judge visited for a while. The twins quickly found a place in Barbara's heart, as she helped clean them up, got them into fresh pajamas and then into the newly-made beds.

"Can you watch them for a few minutes, Babs?" Rusty asked.

"Sure, I'd love to. You go ahead, we'll be just fine," she said as she smiled down at the twins.

Sundance went down to the gift shop and spotted two Raggedy Ann dolls. They were not quite identical, which made them perfect for the twins. Going out to his truck, he pulled out his briefcase and found two homing devices that would be effective to within five miles. Opening up the dolls, he inserted one device into each of them and sewed them back up. Returning to the hospital room, he gave each girl one of the dolls. "As long as you keep these dolls with you, I'll be able to find you. So I want you to promise me that you will keep them with you all the time, okay?"

"I promise," both girls chimed.

"We think the Angel gave us a good new daddy," said Tracy.

"Well, thank you," said Rusty, grinning at them. "I think she gave me two good daughters, too; and I'll keep all my promises to her."

Barbara tucked them into their beds and kissed them goodnight. "We'll be back first thing in the morning," she promised.

"I may need your help picking out new clothes for them," Rusty told her. "I haven't done much shopping for little girls, and I want them to have a swell wardrobe."

"I'd love to," she said. "I just love to shop, just let me know when. Goodnight, try to get some sleep. See you in the morning."

"Goodnight."

Following Barbara and the Judge out of the room, he turned towards the nurses' station to get a cup of coffee for himself and some apple juice for the twins, in case they woke up and were thirsty. When he got back, they were both sleeping soundly, holding onto their Raggedy Ann dolls tightly. He bent over each of them and kissed them on the forehead, then went over to the big easy chair. As he watched the news and then a movie, the hectic and emotional day began to catch up to him and he drifted off to sleep.

22

Rusty slept fitfully, waking up periodically to check on the twins. He was relieved to see that they were sleeping more peacefully than the night before. About five A.M., a nurse came into the room. With some primitive instinct working, Sundance flew out of the chair. *Something isn't right.* He looked at the nurse, and didn't recognize her. She had a hypodermic needle in her hand and was about to give Stacy a shot. *What is she doing? They aren't on any medication anymore!* Flying at the nurse, he knocked her to the floor. She was still holding the hypodermic needle in her hand. Sundance grabbed her hand and bringing it over to her other arm, he shoved the needle into her arm and pushed down the plunger. In less than a minute, the nurse lay dead on the floor.

The noise of the tussle had awakened the girls, and they both started crying hysterically. Sundance rushed over the beds, picked them up and started hugging them to calm them down. "It's okay, you're safe now." Putting both of them back into their bed, he called for a nurse.

The regular morning nurse rushed in to see what the ruckus was about. Taking in the scene, she asked, "What's going on here? What happened?"

"Do you recognize this nurse?" he asked her.

"No. What's wrong with her?"

"She was about to give Tracy a shot, and I yelled out to her to stop, because I knew the twins weren't on any medication. She turned suddenly and slipped, and the needle went into her arm. I guess the pressure of her hand pushed the plunger down when she fell. Can you get a doctor?"

The nurse ran out of the room, in search of a doctor.

Sundance carefully searched the body on the floor. It was clean except for a small two-inch .38 pistol, tucked into her waistband. Removing it, he put it inside one of the plastic bags the Raggedy Ann dolls had been in and put it in his pocket. Then taking off the hat, he studied her for clues as to who she was. Suddenly, he recognized her as the Scarlet Tart, a Russian operative—one of the better ones. *Why do the Russians want the twins dead? How did they find us? There wasn't any reason for them to connect me to the twins. I'll have to talk to Smokey about this. I dare not leave them, even for a moment, now.*

The doctor came in, and Rusty gave him the same story he had given the nurse. "Can you get whatever was in that needle analyzed? I want to know what the hell she was trying to give my girls."

"We'll take care of it. On behalf of the hospital, I'm sorry that this has happened." The police arrived then, and the body was taken to the morgue.

The Judge and Barbara walked in then. "What the hell is going on?" the Judge asked.

"Someone has just tried to kill the twins," Rusty told them. "I have to make a phone call, can you stay with them, and lock this door? Don't let anyone else near them."

"Go ahead, we'll keep a close eye on them."

Going out of the hospital to the phone booth on the plaza, Rusty called Smokey and told him what happened. "We need to get this situation under control, have you come up with anything yet?"

"Nothing yet, Sorry."

"Well get some more feelers out," Rusty told him. "Why would a Russian operative try to eliminate the twins? And how did they connect them with me?"

"The mystery deepens. I can't figure out what this is all about yet."

"Well, I think they may have either witnessed something or

have possession of something. It's the only thing that makes any kind of sense. The question is—what?"

"Keep your eyes open, and I'll get more operatives on this," Smokey said, "Meanwhile, Jake Gunner should be down there in a couple of days."

"Great, with Garth not due back for another week or so, I can really use the help. This situation is escalating, there's no telling what might happen next. I need to get them back to my ranch, where there is more security. Ring me if you find out anything." Hanging up the phone, Rusty headed back into the hospital and up to the girls' room. Taking the Judge and Barbara out of the room and down the hall a short way, he started explaining a little bit of what was going on. Suddenly he heard both girls start screaming and all three of them rushed back into the room as if there were a fire. Sundance was the first one on the scene, and saw a woman holding both girls, coming toward the door with them. He leaped towards her and snatched her by the neck with one of his massive hands and had his 9mm at her head. "Drop the girls, very carefully." She complied. Her feet were about a foot off the floor, and he could see the fear in her eyes. He motioned the girls to stand behind him, and set the woman back down on the floor. "Who are you and why are you kidnapping my daughters?"

"I'm a social worker, and there has been a report from one of the nurses that you have been abusing these girls." Then she saw the Judge and shakily pointed to him. "He can verify who I am."

"She is who she says," the Judge confirmed. "In fact she has been in my court-room a few times, and is a good social worker. It's okay, Marge, there hasn't been any abuse going on here, except for the abuse of power that head nurse seems to be trying to use."

Letting her go, Sundance said, "Maybe next time you'll check with the doctor in charge, instead of taking the word of one nurse. You'll avoid lots of problems."

Apologizing, she left the room to find the doctor.

"Boy, that Guardian Angel knew what she was talking about when she said the road ahead was going to be rocky," Rusty said to the Judge. "I have no idea how to be a parent in simple times, and these aren't going to be simple times."

Barbara had gotten the girls dressed by the time they returned to the room, and a few minutes later Dr. Brown came in to give them one last check up. "Well, it's a miracle, but they seem to be well on their way to a full recovery," he said. "I took care of the social worker, she won't be back. I'll have to see what I can do about that nurse. I'll see you all soon, stay healthy." Grinning, he handed each of the girls a lollipop and shook Rusty's hand before leaving.

Looking at his two new daughters, all Rusty could think was, *What's next?*

Part VI

Working It Out

23

As the whole family was about to walk out of the hospital room for the final time, the phone rang. "I'll get that," Rusty said and walked over to the phone.

"Hello?" After finding out that it was Jake Gunner on the other end, he covered the mouthpiece and said to Barbara, "Can the two of you go ahead with the twins? I'll catch up to you downtown."

"Okay. I think we'll head over to the mercantile first and pick up some clothes and other items for the twins. Then we'll head over to the Gift Gallery, they have some neat stuff; so if you don't find us at Anderson's, check there." Leaving Rusty to his phone call, the four of them left the room, the twins chattering excitedly about the upcoming shopping trip.

"Jake! You barely caught me, how'd you find me?" Rusty asked.

"When I couldn't reach you at home, I called Smokey. He said I could probably still reach you at the hospital. Is everything all right? Are you sick?"

"I'm fine. I'll fill you in when you get there. Where are you now?"

"I'm at a Sambo's coffee shop, about an hour from the turn off to Highway 20, in just past Santa Rosa, but I'm not sure of which way to go from there. I figured I'd call you now, while I was already stopped for breakfast."

Getting a mental picture of where Jake was, Rusty started giving him directions to the ranch. "When you get to Highway 20, go left, heading west. When you see a sign for a campground on the right, go a little over a mile further, and you'll see a small road on the left. Turn there and follow that road for about twenty minutes, you should see a sign that says Kincade Ranch. Make a right turn and go up to the gate and ring the buzzer. If I'm not there, I will be soon. My sister is shopping for the twins right now, then we'll be heading home."

"What twins?" Jake asked.

"That's the long story I'll fill you in on later. Are you ready to have those carpentering skills I've heard so much about, put to the test?"

"Absolutely; I'm looking forward to it."

"I may need to test your espionage skills as well. I'm up against a hell of a puzzle."

Jake laughed. "Smokey didn't tell me I was coming up to have fun too."

"I'll give you the details soon. See you in about an hour and a half." Hanging up the phone, Rusty took one last look around the room, left the hospital and headed over to Anderson's Mercantile to catch up to his family. *What a nice sound that has—"my family." I like it.*

When he got there, he found Barbara and the twins having a blast trying on different outfits. The Judge was sitting in a chair watching it all with an amused expression on his face. Going over to him, he said, "Mind if I join you? This seems to be the safety zone."

Laughing, the Judge said, "Grab a chair!" It was about a half hour before the girls and Barbara were satisfied that they had everything they needed, and Rusty stood up and went to the register to pay the bill.

Once they were outside, Barbara said, "That was fun. Shall we go to the Gift Gallery now?"

"I think that is probably enough for now," Rusty said. "Let's save that for later. I'm sure these two hooligans will be passing out sooner than they think."

"Okay, we'll be up in a couple of weeks to see how you and the twins are doing. Call us if there are any problems."

"Thanks for everything," Rusty said. "I'll keep you posted." Then, loading everything into the back of the camper, he put the girls in the cab, belted them in, and went around to the driver side. Soon they were headed home.

Stacy looked up at Rusty and asked, "Are we going home now?"

"Yes, we are. You're going to your new home with your new dad. You can call me Dad or Daddy from now on. Okay?"

"Okay," said Stacy.

"Okay, Daddy," said Tracy. "I think you will be a good daddy and we love you."

"Well I love both of you too, punkin'."

"How much do you love us, Daddy?" asked Stacy.

"More than all the stars in the sky and grains of sand on the beach."

"That sure is an awful lot of love," Stacy commented seriously.

"It sure is."

24

Rusty and the girls had been on Hwy 20 for about five minutes, when they saw a lot of CHP cars on the side of the road. The officers had their weapons drawn, and were excited about something. Rusty stopped the truck and started to get out to see what was going on.

"Stay inside the truck," one of the officers told him.

Continuing to exit the truck, Sundance pulled out his FBI badge. "Do you need any assistance?" Seeing his badge, the officer stepped back allowing Sundance to approach the scene. "You girls stay here, and keep your heads down."

"Okay, Daddy," Tracy answered for both of them.

Sundance headed toward the excitement, and as he approached he saw that the officers were pointing their weapons at a man that stood about six feet, six inches tall, weighing about 320 pounds—all muscle. He had sandy hair and powder blue eyes that were twinkling in amusement. He had an average nose, squared off chin and a big smile.

"It looks like you found me sooner than we expected," the man called out to him.

"Gunner! What kind of trouble are you in now?" Looking over at the officer in charge, he asked, "What's going on?"

"He was pulled over for speeding and the officer noticed he was carrying a weapon."

"Didn't he show you his badge?"

"Yes, but we're checking him out," the officer explained.

Rusty recognized most of them, and looking around, he spotted Geri. "You all sure do have a strange way of welcoming fellow officers of the law, Geri! Come on over here, I want to introduce you to that friend of mine!"

The other officers slowly put their weapons away and started drifting off. As she approached them, Rusty said, "Geri, I'd like you to meet Jake Gunner, also known as the Cowboy. Jake, this is Officer Abbott."

Jake bowed deeply. "Pleased to make your acquaintance ma'am," he drawled.

Taking in Jake's blue jeans, western style shirt, riding boots and cowboy hat, Geri laughed and said, "Well I can see why they call you the Cowboy. Are you sure you're in the right part of the woods for your outfit?"

"Ma'am, I'll have you know that this is typical dress code for where I come from in Texas," Jake said in mock stiffness.

"Well, it suits you just fine. I like it," Geri reassured him.

"I'm going to be in the area for a while," Jake said, "If you aren't otherwise committed, maybe we could go out some night when you're free."

"How about tomorrow night?" Geri handed him one of her cards with her home address and telephone number on it.

"It's a date then, I'll see you tomorrow night at seven." Jake smiled and waved to her as he went back to his car.

Rusty went over to Sergeant Hagg, who was waiting for Geri. "Do you think you and Geri could follow us up to the ranch? I want to get it totally checked out before I get the twins settled in."

"No problem."

Rusty got into his truck. "You girls did real fine. I'm proud of you. Are you ready to go home now?" They both nodded at him happily.

When they arrived at the main gate, Sundance and Cowboy got out of their vehicles and went over to the patrol car. "We need to take a walk around to check things out," Sundance said to Sergeant Hagg. "Geri, can you stay and protect the girls, please?"

"Certainly. We'll be fine," Geri told him, and went to the truck to join the twins.

The three men checked out the surrounding area, and then Cowboy and Sundance checked the gate for evidence of tampering. Finding nothing amiss, Sundance opened the electronic gate and motioned everyone through towards the main house. Upon arrival, Sundance and Cowboy got out of the vehicles. "Sergeant, Geri? Could the two of you please stay here with the girls while we check out the area?"

"Whatever you want," the Sergeant said.

"Cowboy, check out the cottages over to the right, I'll take the ones on the left." After making sure that they were all secure, they met back at the main house. "Check out the back," Sundance told him. "We'll meet in the kitchen." Once the area had been thoroughly checked out and secured, Sundance went back outside. "Come on in," he called out.

The two officers came in with the girls and all the packages from the shopping spree. Taking the packages, Rusty led the twins to their room, Geri followed. "Do you remember this room?" he asked them. "This is going to be your room from now on. This door leads into my room, so if you need me, all you have to do is go through that door." Rusty had originally put that door in as an escape route for him, in case he ever needed it; but it would work well both ways.

Geri started helping the girls put their new clothes away, and the three of them were having a good time, so Rusty headed back to the kitchen for some coffee. While waiting for the coffee to brew, he put together a plate of cookies and poured some milk for the twins. Taking it in to them, along with a TV tray he said, "Why don't you girls have a `Housewarming Tea Party' in your room for awhile. You can set up this tray as a table, and use pillows and the bed for chairs for you and your dolls. The grown-ups need to talk about some serious stuff right now. We'll be in the kitchen, if you need us."

"Okay, Daddy." Tracy said. Stacy looked up at him and nodded her head happily. Then she started piling pillows up for her doll to sit on.

Down in the kitchen, Jake was pouring coffee for himself and Sergeant Hagg. "Would you guys like a cup?" he asked as Rusty and Geri came in.

"Oh yeah," Rusty sighed.

"Ditto," Geri said. "I'm exhausted."

"What in the hell is coming down around here?" Sergeant Hagg asked Rusty.

"Well, I'll explain what I can, but not everything can be discussed at this time. I don't want you and Geri any more mixed up in this than you already are, it could prove to be dangerous for you. You may be great Highway Patrol Officers, but this is way over your heads and expertise. Jake and I will have to handle this one. Garth and Sandy can help when they get home—which will be soon, I hope."

Geri turned to Jake. "I thought you were here for rehab?"

"I did too. It's all news to me, but when duty calls, we can't put it off 'til later. We might not make it to later." Turning to Rusty, he said, "So what's going on, pardner."

"Well, I'm not really too sure myself; this whole thing just kind of dropped in my lap. I don't exactly know what the reasons are for what is going on; but the twins are in real danger, and it's going to require all the expertise we have to try and solve this riddle." Turning to Geri and the Sergeant, he continued. "This isn't to go any further than this room; but to help you understand, I'm going to tell you this. Jake, Garth, Sandy and I are all with the CIA. We have all been operatives, though are currently semi-retired. We stay available for occasional assignments; but due to our various injuries, it's more for our expertise than physical abilities. There are foreign agents here that are trying to kill the twins. I don't know why, and I don't know how they found them here. As near as I've been able to learn from the girls, someone has probably already killed their parents. Then someone tried to kill them at the hospital."

"That nurse!" Geri interrupted excitedly.

Rusty continued. "Yes, 'that nurse.' She was a Russian spy called the Scarlet Tart. She was a very good operative, and the fact that they risked her for this mission, says that they want these girls dead, badly. If you run into any foreign operatives, don't mess with them. They can kill you in a heartbeat and they'll have no qualms about going after your families in order to get you to cooperate."

"I don't have any family around here to worry about," Geri said.

"Neither do I," the Sergeant said, "and I like it that way."

"That's good, but they can go after your friends too," Rusty told them. "I've been keeping in contact with my boss, but so far he hasn't been able to pin down what is going on either. Sergeant, do you think you could keep an extra patrol car around at night? It might deter someone from trying to enter the grounds."

"Certainly. I'll see to it."

"Another thing. Would it be possible for Geri to be on special assignment here for a while, starting tomorrow? I need a woman here that can help guard the twins. They need to be protected at all costs."

The Sergeant looked over at Geri. She nodded her approval. He turned back to Rusty. "I'll make the arrangements. Now, unless there is anything else," turning back to Geri, he said, "I think we should head back to the station now."

As they left, Geri looked at Rusty and said, "I'll see you in the morning. I need to get some things packed and make some arrangements for someone to watch my place."

"Thank you for accepting the assignment."

"My pleasure." Then she looked over at Jake and smiled.

After they left, Rusty said, "I sure am glad I'll have you and Geri around right now. Things will be even better when Garth and

Sandy get back. Those girls are going to need all the protection we can give them."

Going back into the house, Rusty said, "Jake, can you get the security system down from the top shelf of that closet over there, and join us in the living room in a couple of minutes? I'm going to get the girls."

"Sure thing."

A few minutes later, everyone was sitting around the security system, and Rusty started explaining it to them. "See these lights? Well, the lights you see now are from the monitoring devices here. When one of us wears it, you'll be able to see just where we are. If there are any bad guys around, or anyone else that isn't wearing one, they show up as the blue lights. Right now none of us are wearing monitors, so we all show up as blue. See how it shows us all sitting in this one room?"

The girls nodded.

"When bad guys sneak over the wall, an alarm will sound. That's when everyone puts on a monitor. Then you can see where everyone is compared to where the bad guys are. Okay?" Rusty could tell that Jake didn't understand why he was explaining all this to a couple of five-year-olds, but *you never know. Better safe than sorry.*

After the explanations were done, Jake headed back into the kitchen, "I'm gonna rustle up somethin' to eat. Anybody else hungry?" A chorus of consent followed him from the room.

Rusty let the twins try out the monitoring devices. He and Tracy put on the devices and went to hide. Then Stacy would find them using the security system. Then Rusty showed them how to use the radio. "If you're ever monitoring this when we have to go after some bad guys, you'll use this radio to tell us where the bad guys are. Just make sure you remember who's wearing what color light." He put the radio and a monitoring device on Stacy, took his off and went to hide. Then Tracy gave Stacy instructions on where to go to find him. They were having fun, but they were learning too.

Dinner was ready in an hour, and Rusty put the security system away, feeling confident that the girls would be able to handle it if they ever needed to. Then they all trooped into the dining room for dinner.

When they were done, and the twins were enjoying a bowl of ice cream, Rusty showed Jake where his room was. "Geri will have the one next door. Garth and Sandy have the first cottage on the right." Leaving him to unpack his things, he went back to the dining room, where the twins were just finishing up. Rusty had them help clear the table and put the dishes in the dishwasher. Then he went into the bathroom and started a bath for them.

After the long day, and a great meal, the twins were exhausted, so after their bath, he helped them get into their new pajamas and took them to their room. After saying their prayers, they jumped into the double-size bed, and he tucked them in, kissing them each on the forehead. "There's a little night light over next to the closet, but if you get scared, you can come sleep with me, okay?" They both nodded up at him. *It sure is great being a Dad,* he thought.

Then he turned out the light and headed out to see how Jake was coming along. "Everything okay?"

"Everything's great! Thanks so much for having me."

"My pleasure, would you like to see the workout room?"

They headed to the workout room. "I usually work out first thing in the morning, if you'd like to join me."

"I'd love to, this is impressive. Just knock on my door in the morning on your way by. I'll join you."

"Well, I'm off to bed, it's been a long day. Good night." Rusty headed back to his room and practically fell into bed. About halfway through the night, he woke to the sound of pitter-pattering little feet. Then the twins were snuggling up next to him and fell asleep. Everyone slept very soundly after that.

25

It was about six in the morning when Rusty woke up. Being careful not to wake the twins, he slid out of bed and quietly got into his workout clothes. He knocked on Jake's door on his way to the workout room, and Jake joined him in about five minutes. After a hard workout, they each had a hot shower and headed to the kitchen. Rusty put some coffee on and Jake started breakfast. Rusty went to get the twins up and ready for the new day. He had lots to show them.

As they were eating the buzzer from the gate sounded. Heading over to the gate phone, he heard Geri say, "Good morning, would you be so kind as to let this freezing officer in?"

"Come on up, the coffee is on." He hit the buzzer and headed to the front door to welcome her. When he opened the door to watch her drive up, he saw not one but two cars come through the gate. As they got closer, he discovered that the second car was Garth and Sandy's. What a great morning this was starting out to be.

When they arrived, everyone started talking at once. Jake and the twins came out and added to the pandemonium. Jake gave both Garth and Sandy bear hugs and said, "It's great to see the two of you again. It's been too long!"

The twins were all excited, and Rusty tried to get the introductions made. Once things had calmed down some, Rusty said, "So who wants coffee? Is anyone hungry? Follow me," and he led everyone to the dining room and started taking orders.

After breakfast, while the adults were finishing their coffee and the twins were sipping on cocoa, Rusty decided it was a good time to get everyone caught up.

"Now that I have all the players here, I need to set up the game plan and figure out who will be responsible for what. Geri is directly responsible for the twins. She will protect them at all costs." Geri nodded. "Sandy and Garth, I'd like you two to be in charge of protecting the left side of the property. Make sure everything is in order—the alarm is working properly, the fences are intact, etc. If the walls are breached, that is the side you will handle." They both agreed.

"Jake and I will do the same with the right side of the property. This way, if something happens, we will know where everybody is. If everybody sticks to their responsibility, we won't have to worry about distraction decoys.

"For now, Geri will keep the children in the safest part of the house, so she can easily defend them if she has to. Garth, Jake and I will be building a tree house in the big oak out front. I have already ordered the materials. The whole structure will be both fire and bullet proof, and it will have all the amenities installed. The twins will know what they can and can't use. Also, I will put together another control box up there so Geri and the twins can monitor the battle field, if necessary."

The twins were so excited about the tree house, that they jumped up to give their new dad a big kiss and started chattering about all the things they wanted to have in it.

"Calm down, girls," Rusty told them. "There are going to be ground rules that must be obeyed. The rules are to keep you safe and if one of us tells you to do something, do it as fast as possible—I don't want to lose you; so promise me you'll obey the rules and all of us, okay? This is not just a tree house to play in; it's a tree house that will protect you." They promised. Rusty turned back to the others and continued. "Our main purpose is to protect the twins, even if it means our lives. Someone is after them for some unknown reason and Smokey is trying to find out why. Other than that, we all keep up on our regular work, relax and enjoy the ranch. Garth has fixed up the basement into a rec room with carpet, pool table, pinball machines, ping-pong table and other stuff to amuse ourselves with. And then, of course, there is the workout room. Does anyone have any questions?" No one had any. "Well, let's get going. It's a beautiful day out there."

Part VII

Kidnapped

26

Rusty and crew had been working hard on the treehouse and it looked like it might be completed in a couple of weeks. One day he went to the mailbox to get the mail and found a small package. It contained the two lockets he had ordered a couple of weeks ago. They were made from titanium and on the inside of each golden colored locket was the name of one of the twins and "I love you, Dad." On the other side was a smart heart Rusty unscrewed revealing a small cavity inside the locket.

He placed a homing device inside each one and closed them back up tightly. Examining them closely, he thought, *You can't even tell these open up here unless you're looking for it. The chains look like they will be the perfect length to keep them from slipping them off over their heads.* Now, even if the twins forgot their dolls or were separated from them, he would be able to locate them within up to twenty-five miles in any direction. This range was much larger than the devices in the dolls.

He called the twins in and showed them the lockets. They loved them and he put them on immediately. "I want you to always wear these. Never take them off. You can even bathe in them and they will stay pretty."

Thanking him, they rushed off to show their new presents to Geri. Rusty felt a general feeling of relief wash over him. Now that they were wearing the homing devices, if they happened to get lost of kidnapped, he would be able to find them in a heartbeat.

After they had been gone about ten minutes, he turned on the monitor to test it out. It worked perfectly. Going to find them, he gave a monitor to Geri too, and showed her how to use it. Now she would also be able to find them quickly, as it was her job to keep a close eye on them. She was doing a hell of a good job already.

He had noticed that Geri and Jake were getting pretty serious about each other. *I hope it works out for them. They deserve to experience love the way Sonya and I did.* He still couldn't get Sonya out of his mind. *I wonder if there will ever be someone else I can love as deeply as I love her.* Only time would answer that question.

Three weeks later, the tree house was finished. It looked fantastic, and Rusty knew that that twins would have some wonderful times in it. After it was finished, Jake went to find Geri.

"Hey sweet thing, I've a hankering for some junk food. Do you want to come with me to Willits? We can bring the twins, and get dinner at the Burger King there."

"Sounds like fun, I'll get the twins."

Overhearing the conversation, Rusty called out, "Wait for me." He wrote a quick note to Garth and Sandy, who had gone to the lake to fish, then they all piled into Jake's Lincoln and headed off.

It was a beautiful day, the kind you don't want to miss a single minute of. The twins were having a contest—who could find the most birds.

"I think we're being followed," Jake said.

Rusty checked the side mirror, and saw a powder blue Ford a little ways behind them. "Remember, this is only a two-lane road."

Jake kept an eye on the Ford, but lost it when he turned into Burger King.

After telling Rusty what kind of soda they wanted with their kids' meals, the twins slipped away to get a table next to the window while the adults checked out the menu, deciding what they wanted. When Geri had decided, she told Jake what she wanted, and turned to join the twins. Suddenly she screamed, "Rusty! They're gone!" She turned on the detector she had attached to her belt, looked out the window and saw the powder blue Ford. A man was getting into the driver's seat, she could barely see the twins inside with a woman.

The three of them flew out of the restaurant, Sundance was the first one to get to the Ford. With his huge right hand, he broke the driver's side window and his big fist crushed the skull of the man trying to start the car. Cowboy was at the passenger side with his gun drawn. There were two gun shots, one of the bullets grazed Sundance's head; the other went into the back of the head of the woman holding the twins. She died instantly. Geri pushed past him to get to the twins. She helped them get out of the car, and held onto them as they were sobbing. "It's okay now. Everything will be alright."

By the time Sgt. Hagg and a whole slew of other cops arrived on the scene, Jake had already cleaned up Rusty's wound as best he could. "It doesn't look too serious, but you'll probably have one hell of a headache."

An ambulance arrived shortly after the police did. Rusty sat on the edge of the opening at the back door. "It feels like a swarm of bees is in my head."

The medic chuckled. "I don't doubt it. A half inch to the right and you would have been a dead man. Are you ready to go to the hospital now?"

"I'm not having any of that. I've had enough of hospitals to last at least a few years."

"Well, can we at least give you some morphine for the pain?"

"I don't think so, I need to keep my wits about me; but thanks anyway."

The medic tried again. "Well, at least take some of these for the pain," he said as he handed some pills to Rusty. Giving in, Rusty took a couple of them.

The other medic came around to the back just as a very pale Geri joined them. "I got hold of Dr. Brown and filled him in on what has happened. I told him it is just a flesh wound. He said he would call in some prescriptions to the pharmacy for you and to call him if the pain gets worse or if there are any other problems."

Turning to Geri, he asked, "Are you alright, Miss?" As she nodded, he continued. "Dr. Brown said to keep waking Mr. Kincade up every four hours for the rest of the night. You don't want him to slip into a coma."

Looking at Rusty, she firmly said, "I'll take care of it." Rusty grimaced.

Over at the Ford, Cowboy had taken charge; after going through the pockets of each of the bodies, and putting anything he found into a plastic bag, he turned to the Sergeant. "Sgt. Hagg, go ahead and have some of your men take these bodies to the morgue. They are both foreign agents and some federal agents should arrive shortly to take care of everything." He had already called Smokey to fill him in, and Smokey was making the arrangements.

Sgt. Hagg looked at Jake, grinned and said, "You people seem to accumulate more dead bodies than I ever thought possible in a quiet little town like this. I don't know why or what these people are after, but whatever it is, it must be pretty important."

After all the commotion had died down, they trooped back into Burger King, reordered dinner and sat down to enjoy the meal. The twins kept looking at Rusty worriedly. He reached over and playfully tussled the hair of each of them.

"I'll be fine," he assured them. "In a couple of days, I'll be as good as new." They both smiled up at him, adoringly.

After they were finished eating, Geri took the twins to the bathroom to clean up. "Look at the two of you," she said on their way. "You must be wearing more of your dinner than you managed to get into your stomachs." They all laughed.

Back at the table, Rusty started to talk, but Jake interrupted him. "I know, I know. We broke rule number one. We both jumped out in emotion instead of common sense. If Smokey had seen us, we would both have been chewed out."

Rusty grinned. "Well, at least we had Lady Luck watching

out for us. The only bad thing that happened, is I got grazed by that bullet. If I'd been calmer and in the 'Zone,' it probably wouldn't have happened."

"Well, it is kinda rough to react calmly, when the ones you love have just been abducted. You've never been in that situation before," Jake said.

"I guess you're right. That's just what happened. Well, hopefully we've both learned a lesson." Rusty looked up and saw Geri and the girls coming back to the table. The twins looked a lot better, but would definitely need a bath when they got home. "Is everybody ready to head out?"

It was a quiet ride back to the ranch. The twins snuggled up to Rusty and slept through half the trip. They had had a big day. When they arrived back at the ranch, Garth was out front. When he saw the bandage on Rusty's head, he headed over to the car.

"What the hell happened to you?" he demanded.

Jake led Rusty and Garth into the kitchen, while recounting the events of the day, and started the coffee. Geri took the girls to the bathroom, and ran a bubble bath for them. They delighted in the bubbles—as usual—and between the two of them, they managed to get Geri covered in them. After she got them all cleaned up and dried off, she hustled them into their pajamas and took them to the kitchen to join the others for hot apple pie.

"I just can't figure out what the hell is coming down," Garth was saying as they entered the kitchen. "With all the experience we have between us all, we should have some kind of a clue by now."

Grimacing from the pain of concentrating, Rusty spoke up. "We're missing something somewhere."

"If Mommy was here, she'd know what to do," Tracy said. "Mommy always knows what to do."

Rusty looked like he'd been hit by a truck. "Come to think of it, we haven't heard of any dead woman being found around the time I found the twins. We just assumed she was dead from the twins' story, but maybe we're wrong. I'll make some phone calls in the morning and see if I can come up with anything."

"We should have thought of that sooner," Sandy said.

"Well, things have been a little hectic around here since then," Rusty told her. "We'll talk more about it once the twins are in bed. They look pretty tired."

Geri started taking the girls to their bedroom, but they both started fussing. "We want to sleep in Daddy's bed. He's been hurt and will need some extra love." Laughing, Geri and Rusty headed into his room, had them say their prayers and tucked them into his big bed. Rusty leaned over them and kissed them goodnight. "I love you two. I'll be coming to bed soon. Now go to sleep and have sweet dreams."

Back in the kitchen, they started to develop a strategy for finding the twins' mother.

"If she's alive, you'd think the Russian agents would have found her by now," Jake said.

"They're probably working under the same assumption we are—that she's already dead." Rusty replied. "For all we know she may very well be, and the body just hasn't surfaced yet; but just to be on the safe side, in the morning, we should start checking towns close by for reports of a strange young lady showing up. We can take the twins with us, just to be sure of her, if we find her."

"That's a good idea," Sandy said. "If she's alive, it might shed some light on this whole predicament. . . ."

"Maybe she was hit on the head and has amnesia," Geri offered, "or maybe she's laying low, afraid that whoever is behind all this might try to finish her off."

"Anything's possible," Rusty said. "We'll start making some calls tomorrow morning. Meanwhile, why don't we all turn in and get a good night's sleep."

"This is turning into quite a little suspense thriller," Sandy said. They all laughed and headed off to their rooms.

Part VIII

The Search

27

After breakfast and coffee the next morning, the twins asked Geri if they could play in their new tree house. "Go ahead," she told them, "but don't turn on anything except the television. I'll check on you in a little while." They rushed off.

Meanwhile, everyone else went to work calling the police departments and hospitals in all the towns that were nearby. Shortly after starting his calls, Garth hit pay dirt. Someone in a small town next to the ocean, called Gualala, had found a young lady that seemed to fit the description, and had taken her to the local hospital. She had been treated for a head injury and released.

"Great going Garth," Rusty exclaimed. Then he called the Gualala police department and set up an appointment to come see them. They wouldn't discuss anything over the phone, but agreed to meet with him if he came to town. Rusty wasn't too sure about the tone in the officer's voice, but then remembered that the woman had been hit over the head and left for dead. *They're just playing it safe, can't blame them.* "We'll be up this afternoon," he told the officer. "Thank you."

"Jake? Geri? Can you come with the twins and me to Gualala? Sandy and Garth, I need you two to watch the ranch until we get back."

They all agreed and Geri went to get the twins.

"Don't get their hopes up too high," Rusty called after her. "This lady might not even be their mother."

"Don't worry," she answered, "I'll handle it."

123

28

The next morning, Jake, Geri and the twins were in the Lincoln, ready to go.

"We should be back this afternoon," Rusty said to Sandy and Garth. "Be careful while we're gone, anything could happen."

"We'll be fine. Lots of luck to you," Garth told him. "Now get in the car with everyone else and get out of here. The sooner you figure out what's going on, the better our chances of survival."

"Okay, okay, I'm going." Rusty joined the twins in the back seat, and Jake took off.

It was a fantastic day, warm and sunny. The scenery on the way to Highway 1 was just beautiful. Tracy looked up at Rusty with her big green eyes. "Do you think the lady we'll see today will be Mommy?"

"I don't know, sweetheart. It's a long shot; so don't get your hopes up. Okay?"

"Okay."

"But if it is, why didn't she look for us?" Stacy asked.

"She probably doesn't know where to look, and she might be hiding from the bad man. She could have what is called amnesia, if the bad man hurt her in the head. Then she wouldn't be able to re-member who she is or that she has two little girls." He gave them both a reassuring hug. "Now stop all this worrying; whether it's your mommy or not, the two of you will be just fine. Now watch out the window and look at all the pretty scenery, okay?"

29

Back at the ranch, Garth and Sandy had gone back into the house, Sandy was cleaning the kitchen and Garth was watching television, when all of a sudden the alarm went off. Garth got the control board down out of the closet and turned it on. Three intruders had slipped over the wall and were headed straight for the main house.

"Sandy!" Garth called into the kitchen. "Get into the tree house. It's safer there and it will make it a lot easier to locate the intruders from there. You can then radio me as to where they are!"

They both started running for the tree house. Just before they arrived, a shot rang out and Sandy took a bullet in her arm. Garth quickly helped her up into the tree house. "How bad is it?" he asked.

"It looks like it's a clean shot; it went all the way through. I don't think any bones are broken."

"Put a quick bandage on it. I'll distract the intruders until you can get the board going." With that, Garth took off for the boat dock and a grove of pine trees. He heard a couple of bullets whiz by his head. He felt a lot safer when he hit the grove of trees and climbed up into one of them.

Sandy bandaged her arm as best she could. She was in a hell of a lot of pain, and tried to block it out. She didn't have time to deal with it right now. She turned on the control board and located the three intruders and Garth. "Two of them are coming to the right of you," she told Garth. "Stay in the trees. I'll let you know when they get close enough for you to take care of them."

"Where's the other one?" he asked her. "I don't want any surprises."

"Getting closer to the tree house." Then Garth heard a shot

from the direction of the tree house. Sandy put a bullet in his head, and he never knew where it came from. "Don't worry about him, he's been eliminated."

"Great job!"

"The first intruder is approaching you now. He's about forty feet from you, straight ahead. The other one is trying to circle around you."

Garth spotted the first intruder as he closed to within twenty feet. He put two slugs through the chest and one through the head. Then he quietly dropped from the tree and started circling the second intruder.

"Be careful," Sandy said. "He's about thirty yards to your left."

"I see him." He spirited himself around to a good spot, waited for the intruder to get a little closer, and put a slug in his head. He died instantly.

"I'm on my way back. Keep an eye on the monitor to make sure nothing else is going on." Garth headed back to the tree house, went up, and found the first aid kit.

"You are quite the Amazon, aren't you," he said as he treated her wound. He cleaned it off and put a shot of Novocain into her arm, close to the wound. Then he gave her a couple of pain pills and a glass of water. While her arm was going numb, Garth put on some coffee and said; "I think we'll just stay up here for a while. There's plenty of room, and it's bullet proof." Once the Novocain had taken effect, he started to stitch her arm. It took five stitches to close it up properly, and then he bandaged it all up. "It'll be sore for a few days, then you should be fine."

"Thanks," she said as she curled up on the couch. He gave her a gentle kiss and hug. Then he got up and poured them both a nice hot cup of fresh coffee. *Somehow, coffee always tastes best after a lot of excitement.*

After Sandy had drifted off to sleep, Garth called Smokey to give him the news. "Can you send out one of your clean up crews? I think all three of the intruders were East German assassins."

"What the hell are *they* after? All the other agents have been Russian!"

"I don't know, this is the craziest situation I've been a part of in a long time," Garth told him.

"Where is the rest of the crew?" Smokey asked him. Garth then proceeded to explain what they had come up with so far and what they were doing about it.

"A clean up crew should be there in about an hour or so. They will be arriving by helicopter, so be on the look out for them. Have Sundance call me as soon as he gets back. Get a six-way telephone circuit set up, I'll want input from everyone."

"Will do."

"Oh, keep that control device operating and give Sandy a kiss for me," Smokey continued. "If she has any problems, get her to the hospital."

"I will."

"I'm starting to think I should probably head out there soon. You are all getting more action than all the rest of my agents combined—and you're supposed to be resting."

"The pathetic part is, we don't even have a clue as to why!"

"Something will come up to shed some light on the problem," Smokey reassured him. "It always does."

"Well it sure is taking its time doing so," Garth responded. "Out of all the years Sandy and I have worked for you, this has been the weirdest assignment I've ever been on."

"I'll bet it is. Keep up the good work and keep me posted. Something should break soon."

30

Rusty and company turned onto Highway 1, headed for Gualala.

"I think we're being followed again," Jake told Rusty.

"I know. I noticed them a while ago. Geri, can you see who's in that gray car back there?"

She checked the side mirror. "It looks like three people are in the car, but I'm not sure. The windows are tinted."

"They won't try anything for a while," Jake commented. "They probably want to see what we're up to."

Rusty agreed. "I'm meeting a Sergeant Granger at the police station in Gualala, so they shouldn't be a problem until then, but you'll need to keep a sharp eye out while I'm in there. I know the kids would love to see the ocean, but that will have to wait for another time."

Noticing the twins were getting restless and looked a little worried, Geri whispered to them. "Don't worry, we'll keep you safe."

About twenty minutes later, they pulled up to the police station in Gualala, and Jake parked the car so that they were facing the ocean, giving them a fantastic view. Getting out of the car, Rusty looked around. Gualala was a beautiful quiet ocean town. Perfect for attracting tourism. Geri brought the kids up to the front seat to enjoy the view. They were enthralled with watching the waves breaking as they came to shore.

"I'll be back soon," Rusty told them. Going inside, he approached the Desk Sergeant and showed him his FBI badge. "I'm here to see Sergeant Granger, I spoke to him earlier."

"Have a seat, I'll call him."

Rusty walked over to the front window and noticed the gray

Cadillac that had been following them, parked on the other side of the lot. There were three, maybe four people sitting inside, watching the building and Jake's car. He kept an eye on it until Sergeant Granger walked into the room.

Granger was about six feet tall, and a little on the heavy side, had brown hair and eyes—probably in his late forties. "You must be agent Kincade," he said.

Rusty walked over to him and shook his hand. "Do you see that gray Cadillac over there."

"Yeah."

"How many people do you see inside?"

"I see four people inside," he told Rusty. "Why, what's this all about?"

"Hopefully nothing. Is there anyone else on duty?"

"Just one other police officer. A young kid who has just joined the force."

This situation seems to be getting worse, not better, Rusty thought to himself. "Have him come back to the station and park behind the Lincoln. Do you have any reserves?"

"Three—what's this all about?"

"I can't explain right now, but it is vital that we get to the young lady and make sure she stays safe. Can you get your reserves to the house where she is staying in about fifteen minutes? Once they get there, I want to try to get the girl safely out without any problems."

Granger went to the phone and called everyone in while Rusty kept an eye on the Cadillac. Once everything had been set up, the Sergeant joined him at the window. "Do you have a spare radio I can use?" Rusty asked him, as he saw the rookie pull up behind the Lincoln.

"No problem. Let's go."

As they left the building, Sergeant Granger headed over to his squad car and Rusty walked over to the squad car parked behind the Lincoln. Knocking on the driver's window, he motioned to the rookie to open the window. "Follow us closely," he said as the window came down, "and watch out for that gray Cadillac over there." The rookie nodded, and Rusty got into the Lincoln.

They all departed with Granger leading the way. "It sure took you long enough," Jake commented.

"Sorry about that," Rusty said, "but we have some real problems. There are four agents in the Cadillac, and we have a rookie cop protecting our rear and three reserves that are supposed to meet us at the house. I just don't like the odds right now."

"We'll just have to really stay on our toes then," Jake said, as he looked warily over at the Cadillac.

"You got that right." Turning his attention to Geri, Rusty continued. "When we get to the house, I need you to protect the twins and the young lady there, at all costs. Preferably in a room without windows, if you can find one."

"I'll take care of it," she told him.

Turning back to Jake, Rusty said, "If the situation starts to go wrong, you take the front of the house with Sergeant Granger. I'll handle the back with the rookie." Jake nodded.

Sergeant Granger pulled up in front of a small isolated house. Looking around, Rusty thought, *Thank God there is room to work here, and if those agents try to start anything, they won't have any real place to find cover.* Jake pulled up behind the Sergeant's car, and everyone got out.

Heading back to the rookie's car, which was just pulling up, Rusty went up to the driver's window. "Stay here with the vehicles. If that Cadillac pulls in, let me know by radio." He held up the police radio the Sergeant had loaned him. "If they get out of the car, let me know and then try to make your way to the back of the house and I'll join you there."

The rookie nervously nodded that he understood, and Rusty smiled reassuringly at him before heading toward the house to join the rest of the gang. As they approached the door, it opened a crack.

"What do you want?" asked the voice of an elderly woman.

"It's okay, Mrs. Bettencort," Sergeant Granger reassured her. "These people have come to see the young woman that has amnesia."

"Well, come on in then. I'll go get her."

She led them through the hallway and into the living room. "I'll be right back." She returned in a couple of minutes in the company of a very pretty blonde with high cheekbones and beautiful green eyes like the twins. She was petite—about five feet four inches and her hair was down to her waist. She wasn't wearing any make up, and Rusty found her to be quite attractive.

Mrs. Bettencort started to introduce her, "This is Rose. . . .""Mommy! Mommy!" chorused the twins as the caught sight of her.

The young woman looked at them blankly, not responding. The twins became frightened and grabbed onto Rusty's legs.

"It's okay," he told them reassuringly. "She got a nasty bump on her head, and so she doesn't even know who she is herself, much less who anyone else is."

Peering up his tall frame, Tracy asked him, "Will she ever remember us?"

"She probably will, but we have to be very patient, until she gets better." Rusty turned to Mrs. Bettencort. "Does she have any belongings here?"

She went into the other room to retrieve them.

"Rose?" Rusty addressed her gently. "You're going to be coming home with us now. Your life is in grave danger and we need to protect you while you get your memory back. Do you understand?"

She nodded. The police radio at Rusty's belt suddenly came on.

The rookie's voice came over the radio. "Sir, the Cadillac is here and they are getting out!!"

"Get to the back of the house as fast as possible!" Turning to

131

Granger he continued. "Call in your back-up and have them stay in front of the house!"

Meanwhile, the front door flew open and two shots rang out. The rookie slumped to the floor with a bullet in the head. Looking through the open door, Rusty saw the assailant stumbling, wounded by the rookie's shot. Another shot rang out, from behind him this time, and the assailant clutched his chest as he sank to the ground. He turned and saw Granger was right behind him, holding his weapon out looking for another target. The Sergeant was obviously in a rage and started bolting through the door, but Jake tackled him and Rusty slammed the door closed.

Granger started screaming at Jake. "What in the hell do you think you're doing? They just shot one of my men!"

Jake grabbed him by the shoulders. "You need to calm down or they'll get you next!! We'll handle this calmly and make it out of here. Anger will only get you killed!"

Rusty hustled the women and the twins into a room he had seen earlier that had no windows. He looked at Geri. "Protect them," he said. She nodded and started taking charge as he closed the door.

As he joined the men in the living room, he said, "I'll take care of the back. You two take the front. Granger, are your deputies here yet?"

"They just arrived," he answered in a much calmer voice than he'd had a few minutes before.

"Good, keep them in front of their cars, I'll try to force the agents toward you in the front and we should be able to get a good crossfire going."

As Rusty was approaching the back door, it came crashing down in front of him. He got off two quick shots before ducking for cover behind the dryer. One of the men dropped to the floor. The other two turned around and ran around the side of the house.

"They're coming your way!" he yelled to Jake and Granger.

Suddenly, a long volley of gunfire started up in front. The

three backup officers managed to get both men as they were heading toward the front of the house. Sergeant Granger's voice came over the radio. "Mission accomplished! Good work! Everyone come on in."

Rusty went back into the living room to join the others. As the other officers came in, he congratulated them. "Job well done! Thank you all for your assistance." He saw Jake working on the rookie, looking at Granger, he noticed a blood stain on his shoulder that was getting bigger by the second. "We'd better take a look at that," he said, nodding toward the stain.

Sergeant Granger looked down at his shoulder, shocked that he'd been wounded. Jake had him take off his coat and shirt so he could look at it, while one of the officers called for an ambulance.

Rusty went to the dining room, where the women and the twins were. He found Geri crouched at the door with gun in hand, ready to blow him away. "Relax," he told her. "It's all over." He then led them all into the kitchen so they wouldn't see blood and wounded police officer.

Mrs. Bettencort started making some fresh coffee for the adults and some cocoa for the girls. "Something hot to calm the nerves," she said.

Rusty went to the phone to call Smokey just as the ambulance showed up. "We have found the girls' mother, but there was some trouble. I'll tell you about it when we get back to the ranch. We need to get some good public relations types here as quickly as possible, as well as a clean up squad. And I want a good funeral for the rookie if he doesn't make it and a Medal of Honor for Sgt. Granger."

"I'll take care of it," Smokey told him. "Now, get the hell out of there and call me this evening. In the meantime, I'm going to call in some more agents. We need to get a handle on this situation."

Rusty hung up the phone and went to talk to the officers. "You men go ahead and take the bodies to the morgue. Some fed-

eral agents will be coming shortly to assist you." Jake started helping them remove the bodies from the front walkway as the
ambulance left with the rookie.

Going back to the kitchen, he smiled at Mrs. Bettencort as she
handed him a cup of coffee. She timidly smiled back and carried a
tray of coffee cups out to the other men in the living room.

By 6:00, the house and grounds had been cleared up, the police had all left, and everyone had had time to unwind from all the
excitement. The twins, Rose, Geri and Jake were waiting for Rusty
in the car. Rusty was thanking Mrs. Bettencort for her assistance.
"You've been a real trooper. Don't worry about the damages. I'll
pay for everything." He then pulled out a checkbook from his in-
ner pocket, and wrote her a sizeable check. "This should be
enough and then some; if not, you can call me at the number on the
check."

She thanked him and said, "You'll let me know how Rose is
doing?"

"I sure will. Take care." He then left the house and joined the
twins in the back seat of the car for the long ride home.

31

Once they got on the road, the twins were asleep within five minutes.

"This sure has been one hell of a day!" Jake said. Everyone groaned in agreement. "I sure hope things start to quiet down now."

"I wouldn't count on it yet," Rusty told him. "Rose, do you have any memory at all of what happened to you?"

"No. Mrs. Bettencort told me they found me wandering on the beach. She said my head was bleeding and they took me to the hospital. I just remember waking up in her house in bed."

"Have you had any glimmers of what might be a memory of your life before?"

"No, I wish I did. Are those two little girls really my children?"

"According to them they are. I found them wandering in the hills near my ranch a couple of weeks ago," Rusty said. "We're going to my ranch now. You just relax. It will all come back eventually."

They got to the ranch just before 8:00 P.M. Everyone piled out of the car and into the house. "I'm hungry," Tracy said tiredly.

"Me too," Stacy chimed in.

"I've got some soup warming on the stove," Sandy told them, as she came into the living room to greet them. "Go on into the kitchen with Geri and she can make you some sandwiches to go with it." They complied and Geri followed them. Sandy looked at Rusty and then at Rose, questioningly.

Recalled to his duty, Rusty introduced them. "Sandy, this is Rose. the twins say that she is their mother. She has amnesia and has no memory except for the past couple of days. Can you get her set up in a room not far from the twins?"

"Of course," she said, smiling at Rose. "Right this way. Any luggage?" Looking around she didn't see anything that could be considered luggage. "No? I may have a few things that will fit you. Maybe tomorrow or the next day, we can go shopping for some new items for you."

Rose followed her out of the room.

Jake and Garth came in from putting the car away, and the three of them sat in front of the fire exchanging stories. Rose and Sandy came back in and they all moved into the kitchen to get something to eat.

Geri and the twins were just finishing up. "I'll get the girls bathed and put to bed," Geri told Rusty.

"Thanks. Let me know when they're in bed, and I'll come up for a good night kiss."

"Will do," and they left the adults to their supper.

"Smokey said to call him as soon as we got home," Rusty told Jake and Garth. "While I'm up with the twins, can one of you get the phones set up so everyone can be hooked in for input?"

"I'll take care of it," Jake said.

They had just finished their supper, when Geri called Rusty. "The twins are ready for bed."

He headed back to the bedrooms. "Geri, we'll be having a conference call in a few minutes. Can you join the others in the den?"

"Sure thing." She headed out to the front of the house.

"We want to sleep with you tonight, Daddy," Stacy said.

"Pleeease!" Tracy added.

"Alright," he said and took them into his bedroom and had them say their prayers before tucking them in for the night. "I'll be in shortly. Good night."

"Night, night."

Once everyone was settled in the den for the conference call with Smokey, Jake put the call through. Smokey answered the call. "I was beginning to wonder if you would ever be calling back."

"It was a hell of a day," Rusty said. "We haven't gotten much further in solving this thing, but we did rack up a lot more dead bodies. Someone is pulling out all the stops on this one."

"Do you still have the clothes the twins were wearing the day you found them?" Smokey asked.

"I think so," he replied, then turning to Sandy. "Are they still in the garage with the other clothes you've collected for the Salvation Army?"

"Yeah. I haven't had much time to think about that recently, so they should be right where you left them," she answered.

"I'm sending out a couple of my best 'active' agents to collect them, as well as the clothes Rose is wearing," Smokey said. "They will also be taking fingerprints; maybe now we can shed some light on the whole situation."

"Something serious must be going on," Geri spoke up shyly, "they sure are sending out a lot of agents to this area. Somehow, we need to find out why and how they are getting their information." Jake smiled reassuringly at her.

"You're right about that, Geri," Smokey said. "Damned if I can figure it out with what we have right now though."

"What about that scientist that died of a so-called 'heart attack'?" asked Garth. "Didn't he have a family?"

"He did really die of a heart attack," Smokey said. "Besides, he only had a wife, no kids in the picture. Although, now that you mention it, she had disappeared from the area. We haven't been able to locate her, and she didn't show up at the funeral. Considering what else has been going on, maybe we should look into her disappearance more seriously. Maybe there's a connection."

"The more we twist this around, the crazier it gets," Jake said. "Hopefully, now that we've found the twins' mother, we can find some answers too."

137

"Maybe her fingerprints will give us what we need," Smokey agreed. "The best we can do right now is get a good night's sleep and regroup tomorrow. Rusty, I think you know the two agents I'm sending out to you. Robert Roswell and Paul Sanders."

"Yes I do, it will be good to see them again. I believe we've all worked with them before—except Geri, of course."

Jake, Garth and Sandy all nodded.

"Good, so I'll talk to you tomorrow, after Robert and Paul get there. Good night." Smokey said. Jake hung up the line and everyone headed to their respective rooms—heads full of the day's events and thoughts of possible conclusions.

Part IX

Rose

32

Rusty went into his bedroom and found the twins were still awake, with tears in their eyes. Sitting down on the bed, he gathered them into his arms. "What's the problem here?" he asked gently.

"Mommy really doesn't know who we are!" wailed Tracy. "She's not just playing a game."

"Maybe she'll never know who we are!" cried Stacy.

Rusty held them both close. "It may take some time, but I think eventually, she will remember both of you. It might take a while, after all, she had a serious head injury, so I don't want you two to worry about it so much. You have me, and I'm sure that your mom will learn to love you, whether or not she remembers the past. After all, you're her beautiful, sweet girls."

"Well, we still love her," said Tracy, "and we want her to be our mommy again."

"Look at it this way," Rusty said cheerfully. "You both know she's alive now. Yesterday you thought she wasn't. Things are better already, aren't they?"

They both nodded seriously.

"And I noticed that she kind of knows you from somewhere, but hasn't been able to put it all together yet," he reassured them. "Maybe being around you will help her remember more quickly. We can also say a special prayer to help her remember. Believe it or not, prayers do help all of us a lot. So let's dry those eyes, give me some good cuddles and then get some sleep, okay?"

The twins both nodded and immediately started saying a prayer for their mother. By the time Rusty was ready to crawl into bed, they were both sound asleep. *That Rose is a very pretty lady. I'd better give her time to work on getting her memory back though.* With that thought, Rusty joined the twins in slumber.

33

The next morning was uneventful. As everyone finished breakfast, Rusty, who was sitting next to Rose, gently asked, "Have you remembered anything yet?"

"No," she quietly answered. "The girls have said they want to show me their tree house. Is it safe?"

"Absolutely," he reassured her. "We built it to be accessible to both the girls and the adults. It is probably one of the safest places you can be, around here. Go ahead and have fun. we'll be doing chores around the main house area if you need us, and Geri is always within earshot of the twins. Maybe when you're through at the tree house, the twins can show you the lake. Just be sure to let Garth know, and take Geri with you. Later I'll take you on a tour, if you'd like."

"That would be nice."

Rusty and Jake spent the day cutting back the overgrowth surrounding the main house and the road up from the front gate. Garth did the same around the cottages. The day went pretty quickly, and at around 5:00, Robert and Paul showed up at the gate, just as Rusty and Jake were finishing up in that area.

"Have you got some food for a starving man?" Robert asked them through the gate bars.

Jake laughed. "Same old jokester, aren't ya? Come on in, I'm sure we can rustle up some grub for ya."

Rusty looked at the two of them in mock seriousness, and then turned to Jake. "I don't know about that Jake. Do you think we should? They look pretty disreputable."

"If we don't take pity on them, who will?" Jake responded.

"Oh please mister, please; we're wasting away to nothin'," Paul pleaded, joining in the fun.

"Well, I guess so." Rusty smiled and went to unlock the gate so they could come in. "How are you guys doing? Any trouble finding the place?"

"Not really, but the strangest thing happened," Paul said. "I would swear we were followed here form the Oakland airport. But that doesn't make sense! How would anyone know we were coming, where we were flying in to, and what time we would be arriving? I could be wrong, but I kept seeing what looked like the same three cars off and on behind us; like they were taking turns in order to not be obvious."

"The ways things have been going around here, I wouldn't be a bit surprised," Rusty told them. "I'm starting to think our phones tapped. I'll check out the lines on this side before we call Smokey to let him know you've arrived. In the meantime, let's head up to the house for some dinner." They all climbed into the car and went up to the house, the gate closing behind them.

As they arrived at the house, Geri, Rose and the twins were just arriving as well. They all looked very excited. "Look., Daddy!" Stacy called. "Come see all the fish we got at the lake!"

"I caught the most hugest one, Daddy!" Tracy bragged.

Rusty went to see the fish in the bucket Geri and Rose were both carrying. "My goodness. Looks like we can have fish for breakfast!" Reaching for the bucket, he said, "Let me take that for you, it looks heavy." The women gladly handed it over.

Garth came over having finished up the area around the cottages and the path to the lake. "Is anybody hungry? Sandy came out awhile back saying dinner would be ready about now."

"Yeah! We're starvin'!" Tracy exclaimed, and the twins went running into the house.

"Don't forget to wash up," Rusty called after them, laughing. "Shall we join them, ladies and gentlemen?" Everyone trooped into the house in good spirits. Rusty took the fish into the utility room and placed the bucket in the sink, where he and the girls would clean them after dinner.

Sandy had made a huge lasagna and green salad for dinner. There were lots of oohs and aahs as she brought them to the table. "That sure does look and smell wonderful ma'am," Jake said.

"Yes indeedy. Just what a starvin' man would fantasize about," Robert drawled.

Sandy blushed at the compliments and sat down at the table. Garth started serving up the lasagna and passing the plates around the table, Rusty served he and the twins salad and then passed it on to Rose.

The room grew very quiet for the next few minutes, while everyone enjoyed the food, taking the edge off of their hunger. "This is just great, Sandy," Geri said. "I've got to get your recipe for it."

"Thank you, I'll have to try writing it down for you, my Grandmother showed me how to make it when I first got married; I don't think it's ever been written down."

"I hate to change the subject," Rusty spoke up, "but we seem to have a problem. Robert and Paul think they were followed from the airport. I'm guessing our phones are tapped. There have been too many close calls. Garth, after dinner, could you check out the equipment on our end? After that, we'll give Smokey a call. We'll give him a false itinerary for Robert and Paul with enough code so that he'll know something is going on and let him know to check out the equipment on his end. We should also have some tech guys check out the entire line, so we know we have a secure line again."

"I'll take care of it," Garth said.

"Is there any dessert?" Tracy piped up.

Sandy smiled at her. "I have a big carrot cake in the kitchen. Shall I go get it?"

"Yes please!!" the twins both exclaimed happily.

"Can you two please clear the plates from the table for me?"

"Okay."

Taking the lasagna with her, Sandy went into the kitchen to

get the cake. Geri followed her with the salad bowl and started making coffee. While it was brewing, Sandy put the lasagna away and Geri poured the girls both more milk to go with the cake. Rose and the twins came in with all the plates and carried them over to the sink.

"I'll take care of the dishes, Sandy," Rose said.

"Why, thank you, Rose, that's sweet. The dishwasher is right over there, next to the stove."

While Rose rinsed the plates and put them into the dishwasher, the twins carried small plates out for the cake. Sandy was close behind them with the cake, and started cutting and serving it as soon as she reached the table. A couple of minutes later, Geri showed up with the coffee and Rose with the glasses of milk.

"Robert, Paul—I think I'm going to have you stay here tonight instead of going to the hotel in Santa Rosa," Rusty said. "With the way things are going, I wouldn't be surprised if some agents are waiting for you there, in order to intercept your delivery to Smokey of the clothing and fingerprints. I'll show you your rooms later."

"Sounds good to me," Robert said. Paul agreed.

"Jake, I need you and Geri to go into town and fill in Sergeant Hagg with what's going on. I'll call Smokey and let him know what's going on. I'll use code to keep our `friends' from understanding."

"Sure thing, Rusty," Jake replied. "Afterwards, I think we'll stop in at the Black Bart Bar and Grill; maybe I'll spot some of our `friends' there." He and Geri got up from the table to leave. "We'll see you in a few hours."

When the girls had finished their cake and milk, and Rusty had finished his coffee, Rusty said, "Okay, girls, successful fishermen always clean their catch. This way if you please," and he led them toward the utility room.

Meanwhile, Robert and Paul went with Sandy and Rose to get her clothes and the twins clothes. Then they set up the equipment to scan Rose's fingerprints and eye retina. "Okay, that should do it." Paul said cheerfully. "We'll take this file and the clothes to Smokey, and hopefully, by the end of the week, we should know who you are."

"I think I'll go help clean the fish," Rose said, and went to join Rusty and the girls.

"Well, hi there," Rusty greeted her, with a big smile.

"Hi. I figured since I caught some of those fish, maybe I should be cleaning them too," Rose told him shyly.

The twins were looking at each other wide-eyed and giggled. "Oh goody," Tracy said. "We already cleaned bunches of them, and we're tired."

"Yeah," Stacy agreed. "Can we go now, Daddy?"

"Okay, you little monsters, you can go watch some T.V. until it's time for your bath," Rusty grinned at them. He hadn't missed that little interplay between them. "Behave yourselves!" he called after them as they ran off whispering and giggling to each other.

"Kids," Rusty said, shaking his head. Then he and Rose finished cleaning the fish together, laughing.

As they finished up, Rusty said, "Guess I'll go give the twins their bath now."

"I'll do it, if you'd like," she said shyly. "Maybe it will help me get my memory back."

"It's worth a try," Rusty agreed. "Good luck. Tell the twins I'll be up to tell them a good night story."

"I will, thanks."

Meanwhile, Garth showed Paul and Robert down to the basement for a game of ping-pong.

"This is quite a rec room you've got here," Robert said. "We could live down here for weeks and not get bored."

"Thanks," Garth said. "That's what I was working toward."

147

34

Back in the den, Rusty gave Smokey a call. "Hi! When it rains it pours. There's been quite a bugaboo going on today. The twins found a couple of nervous rabbits this afternoon. Looked like they'd been chased quite a-ways."

"Really?"

"They want to keep them, but I think it should only be for a night or two; give them a chance to fatten up; then I think I'll take them to an area outside of town I've seen. They should be able to find a home in no time. In the meantime, we'll try to find what was chasing them. Do you now anyone experienced with predators?"

"Actually, I do have a guy that enjoys that kind of thing, and he's overdue for a vacation. His name is Steve Conway; I think Jake knows him. I'll see if he's interested.

"Maybe he could check the area out and track down whatever it is. It would be a big help."

(*Translation: Paul and Robert arrived and think they were followed. They are going to stay here for the next couple of days, and then fly out using the Willits airstrip. Can you get someone out here to check the phone lines?*)

"Now, on to business," Smokey said. "Did Robert and Paul make it safely?"

"Yes, we just finished dinner. They have what they came for, and will be leaving for the hotel in Santa Rosa soon."

"Good. By the way, Rusty, I've been meaning to talk to you about getting your phone system upgraded. We've made quite a few improvements since yours was installed. I'll see if I have someone available to come out and check yours out. I'll call you when it's set up."

When he was done talking to Smokey, Rusty went to tuck the twins into bed and read them a story. Rose was just finishing putting them into their pajamas.

"You look like a natural," he told her approvingly.

"I'm just following my instincts," she said. "I think I'll go to bed now. Good night."

"Good night, sleep well."

"Night, night, Mommy," the twins chorused.

"Night, night, girls." Rose turned and left the room.

Smiling at the twins, Rusty asked, "So, how did it go?"

"Almost like it was before," Tracy said happily.

When the twins had finished saying their prayers, Rusty asked, "So what kind of bedtime story do you two want tonight?"

"Uncle Wiggily!" the girls both chimed.

"Here it is, Daddy," Tracy said. "We picked it out already. It's the one where he's washing the dishes and dropping them."

Rusty settled down between the girls and started reading them the story, until they fell asleep. After gently extricating himself, he went to the kitchen to get some coffee. Jake and Geri arrived just as he was sitting down at the table with Sandy.

"Well, everything is set up," Jake said, as they came through the door. "Sgt. Hagg should be here around eleven-thirty to give you the details. I didn't notice anyone at the bar that seemed out of place, so they must be laying pretty low."

"Thanks," Rusty said. "The rest of the guys are in the rec room, Rose and the kids are in bed."

"I think I'll go unwind in the rec room," Jake said. "Geri?"

"I think I'll stay up here and have some coffee and some more of that cake. I'll see you in a while." After she watched Jake leave, she continued. "There goes one of the finest men I've ever met."

Rusty smiled. "I thought you might think so."

"When I joined the CHP, I never dreamed I'd get involved in this type of intrigue."

"When you hang around with this group, anything can hap-

149

pen. Do you think it's something you might want to be involved with on a permanent basis?" Rusty asked. "It can take a toll on you, after a while."

"I'm sure it can," she readily agreed. "I'm enjoying the adventure of living the `spy life', but I would probably get tired of it after a while."

"There's a lot of pride in accomplishing something good and positive for the United States," he told her. "It does have a big down side though, you can lose a lot of close friends, and the action can shorten your own life span, if you're not extremely careful. During the span of being an agent, it's best not to have any close social ties, and that leads to a lonely existence. So there's a good and bad to being an agent. The part I like best is the adventure and outsmarting my opponents. It takes a lot of cunning and expertise to accomplish your assignments. But, your job is probably dangerous enough, plus you can keep that big handsome hunk you've been running around with."

Part X

Saving the Rabbits

35

Sergeant Hagg arrived at the Kincade ranch around 11 P.M. to let him know everything was set to go and to give him the details for the next day.

"Thanks for all your help Sarge," Rusty said. "I'll need to contact my boss to let him know what's coming down."

"Has Rose remembered anything yet?" the Sgt. asked.

"Not yet, but we have hope. She is feeling more comfortable with the twins."

"That's good, but it would shed more light on things if she could remember something."

Rose walked in just then. "I wish I could remember something, Sergeant. Everything is still a big blur."

"Don't worry about it," Rusty reassured her. "It will all come in its own time." Every time he looked at her, he realized he was falling for her. *She may not be Sonya, but she's a very close second. I'll have to control myself and give her a chance to recover her memory first, though.*

Sandy could see what was happening, and when she passed Rusty she whispered, "Bide your time, and things will have a good chance of working out."

Realizing he had been more transparent than he'd intended, he responded. "You're right."

Noticing the exchange from across the room, Garth came over. "So what's the big secret?"

"None of your business, Nosey," Sandy teased him and winked at him. She would tell him about it later in private.

Sgt. Hagg was just getting ready to leave, when the alarm went off. "What the hell is that?!" he exclaimed.

153

"We have more intruders," Garth informed him.

Sandy was already getting the control board down and saw at least twelve to fourteen blue chips. Geri and Rusty ran into the girls' room and grabbed them and then went back to join the others.

Rusty started barking out orders. "Geri, get the twins and Rose into the tree house; use the control board there to track the red team on the right side of the property. Sandy, track this control board from here and watch the house. You'll hand the gold team on the left and middle of the board."

Sandy started to protest. Rusty cut her off. "You still have a wounded arm and I need you on the board." Sandy bit her tongue and helped Geri get the twins and Rose ready to go to the tree house.

"Jake, Robert, Sarge—you'll be the red team. Make sure the women and the twins make it to the tree house and guard the right side of the property. Paul, Garth, come with me and we'll take the left and middle of the property. Let's go!" Everyone jumped into action and was on their way. It took less than two minutes for Jake's crew to get the women and girls secured in the tree house, and then they spread out for the search.

The intruders were wearing night vision glasses, but the Kincade bunch had the edge with the control board, even if they were outnumbered two to one.

Geri turned on the low floor lights in the tree house, so they could see what they were doing without attracting the attention of the intruders. Rose put the girls in the bed that was in the upper level of the tree house. "Go back to sleep now. Everything will be alright," she told them. Going back down to the main level, she decided to make some tea for them both. *I'm all coffee'd out; I hope Geri likes tea.* When it was ready, she put a cup on the table next to Geri, and then made herself comfortable in the rocking chair and began sipping her tea while she watched Geri work the board.

Geri noted that there were seven blue dots approaching the

154

area. "Jake—you've got seven of them coming in. They are starting to get close, so be careful." Suddenly they heard shots. "What's happened?" Geri demanded into the headset, starting to panic. Then one of the blue blips disappeared.

"Settle down, Honey. Panic won't help the situation. We need you focused if we're gonna get through this," Cowboy told her. "Sgt. Hagg shot one of the intruders, but he caught one himself. I don't know how bad, but he's down."

"According to the control board, one of the intruders is gone, so he's probably dead, but all of the red ones are still lit," Geri said with relief. "Wait a minute—there goes another blue blip, but I didn't hear any shots. Is the board malfunctioning?"

"Take it easy, that was me," Robert told her. "I used my knife. I didn't want to give away my position."

Geri took a deep breath. *Shut up, Geri, you're blabbering.* She took a sip of the tea Rose had made her. Smiling at her in thanks. "Okay," she said. "There's two more coming up behind you, Jake."

Turning around, the Cowboy spotted them. "Got 'em." Two shots rang out and both intruders sagged to the ground.

"Two more out," Geri said.

Meanwhile in the house, Sandy was tuned into the gold team on the other board. "Everybody ready? There are three intruders coming down toward the left side of the house, and two more heading straight for the house. There are another six of them staying back at the wall for some reason, so be careful."

"Garth, you intercept the ones heading for the house. Sandy, be prepared to help him out. Paul come with me, we'll take on the other three and hope the six at the wall stay put for now."

Paul spotted the first one coming through the trees toward the side of the house; fired off one shot, killing him, but took one in return in the shoulder. Sundance spotted the other two; they were getting close. He took out one of them with his dart gun. As he fell, the other intruder caught sight of him, and took a shot at him. The bullet grazed Sundance's right hand, causing little damage—*just a little burn.* He fired two shots into the other man's chest, killing him instantly.

Meanwhile, Garth came within range of the other two intruders, who were attempting to get into the house. Firing at the one that was going for the window, he said to Sandy, "Fire a clip through the front door, now!" The man at the window crumpled and Garth turned his attention back to the door in time to watch the man there fall to the ground in the open doorway. Approaching the door, he saw Sandy looking out warily. "Nice work," he complimented her.

"Just like the old days," she said with a grin.

"The six that stayed back have gone back over the wall," came Geri's voice through the headphones. "It looks like the rest have all been accounted for. I show no more blue blips on the control board in either sector."

"Great work, guys," Sundance said. "Geri, I want you, Rose, and the twins to stay up in the tree house for the rest of the night, just in case they try anything else. Everyone else meet me at the house."

When Rusty got back to the house, Sandy was already working on Paul's shoulder. "How is it?" he asked her.

"Nothing serious. I'll just clean it up and give him a couple of stitches. He'll be just fine."

"Robert, can you give Smokey a call, in code telling him what happened and to send out a clean up crew for nine enemy bodies. Garth, come with me; we need to find Sgt. Hagg, he hasn't made it back yet." Rusty and Garth headed out in search of the Sgt.

Approaching a stand of pine trees, they heard a low moan. Drawing his weapon, Rusty motioned Garth to circle around to the other side of the trees, then slowly approached to see who it was. Behind the stump of a fallen tree, he found Sgt. Hagg starting to come to. "It's okay Garth, I found him. Come on in."

Checking him over, Rusty discovered he was wearing a bullet proof vest, which had stopped the penetration of the bullet, but the force had knocked him hard and he must have hit his head. There was a gash and bump at the back of his head. *That's probably why he's been out of it so long. He may have a concussion.*

As he became more coherent the Sgt. looked at both of them, "What the hell happened?"

"Well, keeping it simple, you shot one of the intruders, and he shot you back," Garth said. "Your vest saved you from joining him at the pearly gates."

"You may have a concussion though," Rusty told him. "The gash on the back of your head looks pretty bad, and you were out of it for quite a while." Turning on his headset, Rusty reported back to the house. "We've found him. Looks like he'll be alright, we'll be in soon."

"Darn," Geri responded teasingly. "Just missed an easy promotion to Sergeant."

"It will take a lot more than that for you to get my stripes, Abbott," Sgt. Hagg retorted. They both laughed.

When they arrived at the house, Sgt. Hagg said, "First thing I have to do is call in. I'm in charge of the night crew tonight, and I need to let my second in command know that he'll need to take over."

When he returned from making his call, Sandy went over to him and helped him remove his vest. "My turn," she said. She took a look at where the bullet hit. "You'll have a hell of a bruise for a while and it will probably be tender. I have some aloe vera, I'll go get it."

In a couple of minutes she returned with an aloe leaf and an ice pack. She continued. "This will speed up the healing process if you use it regularly, so you might want to take some with you on your way home in the morning." Then she turned her attention to the gash, washing away the blood, she put some aloe on it as well and then had him hold the ice pack on the bump to reduce the swelling.

157

Once she was done, Sandy went back to the kitchen and came back with some coffee and cups. "Anyone want coffee? Sarge, you shouldn't sleep yet for a couple of hours, we need to make sure your head is okay." Rusty and Garth opted to join them in having coffee; Paul and Robert decided to try to get some sleep since they had to travel tomorrow; Jake decided to go to the tree house and see how Geri and Rose were doing.

About 1:00 A.M., the gate phone rang. The clean up crew had arrived. Rusty and Garth went down to the gait to let them in. "Hi, Rudy," Garth said to the guy in charge. "How are things going?"

"Hey, Garth. You guys have sure been busy. I've been sent here for clean up so much in the past few weeks, I'm starting to think I should get an apartment nearby."

"Hopefully, this won't be going on much longer," Rusty interjected. "Let's get busy, the first group is over here."

The clean up took about half an hour, and the crew left. Garth and Rusty headed back to the house. Sandy was just pulling blankets out of the linen closet when they got there.

"How's he doing?" Rusty asked her.

"He seems to be fine, I've given him something for the pain and I'm just making up the couch for him to get some rest. It's been a long night, why don't you two get some sleep. I'll be along in a minute."

"Sounds good," Rusty said and headed off to bed.

"I think I'll wait for you, Sweetheart," Garth said and went into the kitchen to keep Sgt. Hagg company while he waited.

36

It was 10:00 A.M. and it was an overcast morning. The plans for the day were being discussed over breakfast.

"Sgt. Hagg and Geri will be first in the CHP car, followed by Robert and Paul will be second in their car," Rusty said. "Jake, you and Garth will bring up the rear in your Lincoln. You know what to do if something develops. Flash your lights to the two cars ahead of you to let them know the situation.

"Sarge, if there is any trouble, the four of you need to take off fast and get the hell out of there. Let Jake and Garth handle the problem—that's what they're good at. Your job is to get Robert and Paul to the airstrip and onto the CHP chopper safely. Call in some of your people to take over the rear guard. Make sure they stay out of Jake and Garth's way.

"Robert, you need to keep up with the Sarge at all costs. Sandy and I will stay here and protect Rose and the twins. If we get any more intruders, we'll be in the tree house. We can hold off an army from there if we need to."

Five minutes later, the motorcade left. Just before they reached Willits, Garth spotted a sedan following them. "Looks like we've got company."

Jake flashed his lights and dropped back, allowing the cars ahead of him to speed on ahead. The sedan started to try to pass him, but Jake swerved into their path. "I don't think so, boys," he muttered. They kept trying to get past him, but Jake was having none of that. Finally he forced the sedan to a stop in a turnout. Two foreign agents stepped out of the car and started toward them. Jake and Garth got out of the car and met up with them, keeping a distance of about fifteen feet between them.

Jake recognized both of them, they were fairly new to the business. Looking at them distastefully, he asked, "What the hell do you two want?"

The larger of the two spoke up. "Why, we're here to kill you, Cowboy, couldn't you guess?"

Cowboy laughed. "In your wildest dreams, but if you think you two have the edge, just go for any weapon you have. I guarantee neither one of you will live to tell about it."

"That's alright, the Iceman will love to know you are here. You've been promised to him." Cowboy was a little taken aback. The Iceman was the one that had cost him part of his foot. In return he had taken his left hand. The man continued. "I'm sure the Black Raven would love to accompany him here and take care of Sundance at the same time."

"That showdown is one that we aren't worried about. It'll happen when it happens."

Realizing that they weren't going to get any answers, Garth interrupted. "Why don't you peons get the hell out of here while you're still alive? Make sure you turn around and head in the other direction."

The one doing all the talking nudged the other one and they headed back to the car and got in. As they pulled out of the turnout, they started to turn around and then sharply turned the other way, swerving to go around Jake's car.

Garth took something out of his pocket and threw it underhanded, beneath the car as it started to take off. Grabbing Jake and throwing him to the ground, he yelled, "Fire in the hole!" Suddenly there was a huge explosion and the other car went at least ten feet up into the air, and then rolled down into the ravine.

As Garth helped him up, Jake asked, "What the hell was that?"

"Just a little souped-up grenade I made up," Garth said calmly.

"I think you used a little too much soup," Jake grinned.

Garth cracked up laughing. "It sure was a hell of a good blast, but I have to admit it was a bit strong."

Walking over to the edge of the ravine, they peered over the edge where the car had gone. "There's nothin' left but a few pieces of metal and bone fragments down there," Jake said grinning, as they started back to the car. "You put enough soup in that thing to blow up Mount Rushmore. Do ya think that's wise?"

"It was the only thing to do," Garth answered. "The Iceman doesn't know you're here. I think he and the Raven are trying to take out Sundance so that then they can go after the twins and Rose, at their convenience. If they knew you were here, they would change their strategy. The fact that they don't know, gives us the edge; it also provides more safety for the twins."

"You've got a point there."

The two of them got into the car and took off for the airstrip to reconvene with the rest of the group.

After a couple of minutes, Jake spoke up. "So how long have you been tinkering around with weapons?"

"Well it's always been something I wanted to get into, and since I've been at the ranch, I've had more time to work with them. Some of my creations have even been passed onto Smokey to be added to the CIA arsenal."

"Well that last creation of yours sure came in handy. No one will ever figure out what the hell happened back there."

"That's the idea."

The chopper was on the tarmac when they arrived at the airstrip. Geri ran over to the car and gave Jake a big kiss and hug. "What took you so long? I was getting worried."

Not wanting to broadcast the details, Garth quickly answered her. "We persuaded a couple of Russian agents to travel in another direction. We didn't see anything more of them, so they must have taken our advice." Grinning at her, he continued teasingly, "So were you worried about me too?"

Going around to the other side of the car, she gave him a big hug as well. "Thanks for watching out for my big lug over there," she said nodding her head in Jake's direction.

Bowing Garth answered, "No problem ma'am."

The three of them walked over to join Sgt. Hagg, Robert and Paul at the chopper.

"Do you know the pilots well?" Garth asked the Sergeant.

"No worries there, gentlemen," he reassured them. "I've known them for quite a few years. Good men, both of them. They're getting clearance now, it should be no problem getting them to the Sacramento Airport safely."

As he spoke, one of the pilots gave them the thumbs up and Robert and Paul climbed aboard. Two minutes later they were on their way. Everyone else headed back to the cars.

"I'll see you all later," Sgt. Hagg said to them, waving.

37

"This has been quite an adventure," Geri said, as they headed back to the ranch. "I sure will be happy to see this end so we can all settle into some kind of a normal life."

Jake laughed and said, "Tired of me already?"

"You'll need an act of Congress to get rid of me," she vowed.

Giving her a big one armed hug, he said, "I feel the same way."

They passed the spot where Garth had blown up the sedan, but neither man said anything, as they didn't want Geri to know about it. There was a smoke scorch on the side of the road, but she didn't notice it. It would disappear with the first rain.

When they arrived at the ranch, Rusty met them at the door. "How did everything go?"

"Geri," Jake said, "can you go check on Rose and the girls?"

"Are you trying to get rid of me?" she asked.

"As much as I love you, there are some things that I can't tell you," he said. "Federal business is confidential. What you don't know could save your life. As a Highway Patrol officer, you are in the line of danger enough as it is. I don't want to put you in any more danger than you've already been in. I'll see you soon."

Geri left the men alone and went off in search of the twins, but Jake knew she wasn't happy about it.

Sandy put on a pot of coffee and they all sat down to the table.

"What's this all about?" Rusty demanded.

Garth started telling the story. "Not too far from the ranch, we noticed we were being followed. . . ." He proceeded to outline everything that had happened on the way to and at the airport. " . . . and Sgt. Hagg has known both of the pilots for quite a few years, so things should be fine. We can check with Smokey later to make sure they arrived safely."

"So what do you make of the comments about the Iceman and the Black Raven?" Rusty asked.

"It sounds like they are both in the area. They are probably planning to join forces against you, since they don't know that Jake is in the area. They probably figure that between the two of them, they can take you out, and then they can gather the rest of their forces and storm the ranch, and take out Sandy and me. Then they can easily get the twins and Rose. That's why I decided to take them out. I thought it was better for them to not know Jake is in the picture as well."

"Don't anyone forget," Jake interjected quietly, "the Iceman belongs to me."

"You've got it," Rusty said, "and the Raven is mine."

Nodding, Jake continued, "I don't want Geri to know about this. She has enough worries already."

Rusty, Sandy and Garth all nodded in agreement.

Sandy then spoke up, "Do you think the stuff Robert and Paul took back with them will really shed any light on this situation?"

"We can only hope," Rusty said to her. "How about some lunch. I'll bet everyone is starving."

Jake went to get Geri, Rose and the twins while Sandy started making sandwiches and soup. When he found them, he could tell that Geri was upset. "Don't worry so much, Honey. Everything will turn out just fine. I trust you with my life, but I want you to be safe as possible."

She gave him a big kiss and hugged him. "I just worry that I'm going to lose you. I love you too much and don't want to lose you for anything."

"Well come on into the kitchen for some lunch then, I'm starving."

"We are too," chimed in Tracy. And with that they all trooped back to the kitchen. Lunch was on the table and Sandy was just pouring some coffee for Geri and Rose as they arrived.

"Hey there, all," Sandy greeted them. "Looks like we get to play the waiting game for a while. Let's have some lunch."

"We still have to stay alert," Rusty warned them all. "Anything can happen. If we let our guard down and get complacent, one wrong move could take us all out."

Part XI

Tanya

38

Over the next few weeks, things were pretty quiet at the Kincade Ranch—almost too quiet. Smokey had let Rusty know that Robert and Paul had made it back safely, but he had received no new information from the things they'd brought back with them. He was putting out feelers to see if he could find out what the Black Raven and the Iceman were working on, just in case there was a connection.

Meanwhile, the feelings between Rose and Rusty were definitely heating up, but both of them were holding off due to the circumstances. Rose still had not had any real breakthrough in recollecting her past and Rusty didn't want to take advantage of her illness. Jake and Geri were spending every minute together that they could, outside of their protection duties. Garth and Sandy were enjoying watching it all and were making bets on when the weddings would be. The twins were having the summer of their life, between fishing at the lake and spending time in the tree house.

It was a hot, lazy August afternoon, and Rusty had left Rose and the twins in the living room while he went to get some iced tea for everyone. Suddenly he heard a loud thump and the sound of things falling. Heading out to investigate, he nearly ran over Stacy running the other way.

"Mommy's hurt! She fell down and hit her head!"

Rusty rushed into the living room and over to where Rose was lying motionlessly. Tracy was nudging her mother's arm, trying to wake her up. "Wake up, Mommy, wake up!"

"It's okay, Tracy, I'm here," Rusty said gently. "Why don't

you go stand with Stacy next to the fireplace and I'll get your mom up on the couch."

Tracy went over to Stacy and they held hands tightly while looking on in wide-eyed worry.

After setting up the couch with a plump pillow, and doing a quick examination to make sure Rose hadn't broken any bones, he lifted her up and laid her on the couch. Then he reached over and pulled the quilt from the back of the couch and spread it over her. *Must make sure she's warm. She may be in shock when she wakes up.* "Okay, you two," he said to the twins, "come on over here and sit on the edge of the couch. We don't want her to roll off. I'll be right back."

The girls came over and settled themselves on the edge of the couch, and then leaned over her, hugging her. "You'll be okay now, Mommy," Tracy said. "Daddy's taking care of you."

Rusty rushed into the kitchen and made up a quick ice compress for Rose's head. Taking it back out to the living room, he bent over her and gently put the compress on her head. *It looks like she's hit it in just about the same place she did before. It's gonna hurt like hell when she wakes up.* He leaned in a little closer to get a better look at it and suddenly he felt a sting and his face was burning. Rose had woken up and smacked him good and hard.

Grabbing her hand to prevent a repeat, he yelled in surprise, "Why the hell did you do that?" She just stared at him. "Why did you hit me, Rose?" he asked more quietly.

Garth, Sandy, Jake, and Geri all rushed into the room with weapons drawn. Seeing no one but Rose, Rusty and the twins in the room, Garth asked, "What the hell is going on in here? What's all the yelling about?"

Before Rusty could answer him Rose spoke up vehemently, "My NAME IS TANYA; now LET GO of my hand NOW!!" All eyes turned to her.

Rusty let go of her hand and motioned the others to put their weapons away. *She looks terrified,* he thought as he backed off, giving her some room. Tracy and Stacy jumped off the couch and rushed to join Rusty, each of them grabbing one of his hands.

"It'll be okay, Daddy," Tracy said, looking up at him. "Mommy's awake now."

Rusty reached down and gave her a quick hug. "Thanks, honey."

"Tracy!" Tanya said reprovingly, "that's not your father."

"He is too," she cried. "He's our new Daddy, the guard'n angel said so!"

"It's okay, Tracy," Rusty said quietly. "We'll tell her the whole story later when she's feeling better."

Releasing his hands from the grips of the twins, he went over to the couch and helped Tanya into a sitting position and repositioned the compress. "You should keep the compress on your head. That bump is really swelling. Let me make some introductions. I am Rusty, and the Hole in the Wall Gang over there are Jake, Geri, Garth, and Sandy. Geri is a Highway Patrol Officer and the rest of us are Federal Agents, so you're in safe hands."

Trying to get a grip on reality, Tanya tried looking at all of them, but her head was hurting so bad that she had a hard time grasping everything, so she just concentrated on Rusty, since he was the closest one and seemed to be in charge.

"Does she remember her last name?" Garth asked.

"I don't know," Rusty responded. "Tanya, do you know your last name?"

She tried to remember, but her head hurt too much and she gave up in frustration. A tear started to escape from her right eye.

"It's okay, Honey," Rusty said gently. "Sometimes these things can take a little time. We'll get you something for that big pain in your head, and then let you rest for a while. I'll take that compress now, and we'll reapply it later, okay?"

Picking up on his cue, Sandy went into the bathroom to get the bottle of aspirin. Bringing it back along with a glass of water, she gave them to Rusty.

171

Opening the bottle and pouring out two of the pills, he handed them and the water to Tanya. "Now take these, lay back down, and get some rest. The rest of us will be in the kitchen if you need us." After she took the pills, Rusty helped her lay down.

Turning to the twins, he said, "You two watch out over her. If she starts moving around a lot, one of you come and get me. Okay?"

The twins nodded and then the adults headed into the kitchen.

Geri started brewing some coffee for the adults and put some water on the stove for hot cocoa for the twins to have later. As she sat down at the table, she glanced over at Rusty and saw the mark from where Tanya had belted him. Giggling, she asked, "Did you get a little too fresh?" Everyone else started laughing as Rusty turned beet red.

"Well, she does pack quite a wallop," he admitted. "I'll have to remember that and remember to steer clear when she's angry."

As the laughter died down, Jake turned the conversation to business. "Well, at last we may start gettin' somewhere in unraveling this here little mystery. When Tanya's in better shape, we'll talk to her some more, then we'll get ahold of Smokey and let him know what's happenin'."

Garth picked up the thought, "Maybe her first name, along with whatever else she can tell us, will give him some clue as to who she and the twins are. Then maybe we can make some sense out of all this. She obviously has some memory of her husband, since she knows that Rusty isn't their father." The rest of the group agreed.

"That's part of the reason I left the twins with her while she rests," Rusty said. "Maybe being with them will help jog some more of her memory."

"Have you thought about what might happen when she does regain her memory, Rusty?" Sandy asked.

"What do you mean?"

"Well, she's their mother. You may have some problems claiming the twins as yours and keeping them here."

"You might be right; but, for the time being, I have federal authorization to have them."

"How are you going to explain that to Tanya so that she will accept it?"

"Well since they are all in great danger, protecting them is paramount. I'm sure that Tanya will see the sense in that. I'll worry about the future later, if I need to."

"You're sure gonna have your hands full, pardner," Jake said.

"Don't worry about it, it will all work out just fine. You'll see."

Excusing himself, he went to check on Tanya. As he reached the couch, he heard Tanya turn over on the couch to look up at him.

"Sorry I slapped you," she said. "I kind of freaked out."

"No apology required," he said, "It must have been quite a shock to open your eyes and see a strange man so close to you." He sat down on the edge of the couch at her feet. "How are you feeling?"

"A lot better. Those pills started working a couple of minutes ago. The twins have been filling me in on everything," she said, looking a little embarrassed.

Rusty looked at the girls questioningly. They both looked back, grinning unabashedly.

"Well, you don't need to worry about any of that right now," he said. "Everything is a clean slate as of right now. I'm just so glad you remember the twins and your name now. It's a good start and gives us hope that you will eventually remember everything."

"I want to thank you for finding the twins and taking such good care of them. They told me what happened. I don't know what would have happened to them if you hadn't found them." Rusty could see that just thinking about the possibilities was starting to upset her.

"Take it easy. There's no sense in going there," he reassured

173

her. "I did find them and they are safe—as are you. And you will all stay that way for as long as I'm around—which will be a long time." Realizing he was starting to tread on the custody issue a little too soon, he continued, "We'll talk about all that later."

Reaching out her hand for his, it was her turn to reassure him. "The twins have told me all about the fact that they believe you are their new father. They really love you and you being their new dad is very important to them. We'll work it out."

Sighing in relief, Rusty felt as if a big burden had been lifted from his shoulders. "Well, those two little girls are the most important things in my life right now. I know it may be hard to believe, but the story about the Guardian Angel is true, and their angel had me make a solemn oath that I would protect them with my life. Nothing will stand in my way of keeping that oath at all costs."

He was enjoying the warmth of her hand on his, and was careful not to move. "I may bark out some orders from time to time, but if I do, you need to do what I say. It could be life or death. There have been some pretty nasty agents around here lately."

Shuddering, she replied, "After what I've been through, I can believe it. I will definitely follow any directives you happen to 'bark' my way."

Nodding in approval, he gently removed his hand from hers and then turned to the twins. "Well, it looks like things are going to work out," he said to them and gave them a big hug.

"Supper will be ready in half-hour," Geri said from the kitchen door.

"Well, that should give us just enough time to show you around the house," Rusty said to Tanya. He then gently helped her stand up, and as soon as she felt steady enough, the four of them started toward the back of the house.

When they arrived at Tanya's room, she looked around, opened the closet and asked, "Where did I get all of these clothes?"

"Sandy and Geri took you shopping a few months ago."

"A few months ago?" she asked with trepidation.

Realizing that she was ready to find out just how much time had passed, Rusty said, "Today is August eighteenth."

Gasping, Tanya sat down on the bed hard. "I can't believe I've ben out of it for so long." All of the shocks had finally caught up and began sinking in, and she started to weep.

Rusty went over to the bed and sat down beside her. He put his arm around her shoulders. "It's okay, let it out. Everything must seem so strange, but things will work themselves out." Her head turned into his shoulder and she began crying even harder. He started stroking her hair, comforting her. He enjoyed feeling the warmth of her body against his.

"Why is Mommy crying?" Stacy asked.

"Sometimes things happen too fast for them to sink in right away. Your mommy has been very brave so far, but everything just caught up with her and it hit her hard."

"Oh," she said, just as confused as ever.

Realizing that she was too young to understand. Rusty said, "It's okay, I'll explain it to you better, later."

"Okay."

Tanya was beginning to calm down and pulled away from Rusty. "Thanks for the shoulder. I'd better freshen up some before supper."

Giving her a quick kiss on her forehead, Rusty said, "We'll wait for you in the other room."

Looking at his soaked shoulder, she said, "You might want to change your shirt."

He looked down at his shoulder and looked back at her grinning. "You've got a point." Then he and the twins headed out of the room.

As Tanya walked into the bathroom and turned on the shower, she started to turn things over in her mind. *That big giant of a man is really quite handsome and so gentle. It was nice being held so closely by him. It was like being in a safe harbor. I should*

take it slow though; I don't want to give off a wrong impression.
Finished with her musing, she finished her shower and got ready for supper.

39

Tanya was feeling somewhat better as she sat down to the table and joined the small talk. There was a great smelling roast beef at the head of the table that Garth was carving and serving up. Mashed potatoes, rich mushroom gravy, asparagus, and glazed carrots were making their way around the table. As the potatoes reached her, Tanya reached for the bowl and suddenly gasped, dropping the bowl. Rusty grabbed hold of it and set it on the table. Turning to Tanya, he put his hands on her shoulder. "Are you okay?"

Her face was pale as she answered. "I think I remember the man that took us and hit me with the gun while we were in the car. I was serving the girls dinner—chicken and mashed potatoes—when he arrived."

"Anything you can remember might help, no matter how minor it may seem."

"He was a big man, almost your size and build, with really dark hair. He was wearing a patch over his eye and a nasty scar running down the left side of his face. He also seemed to have trouble moving his left arm or shoulder. He was wearing a big black leather coat. That's all I can remember."

The room had gone silent as she described a man that four of them knew quite well. "You and the twins are very lucky to still be alive," Rusty told her quietly. "You just described to a 'T' a very well known Russian agent, probably the most dangerous assassin in the Russian Secret Service." Turning to Garth, he continued, "Give Smokey a call after dinner. Tell him what we've just learned and let him know that Rose has remembered that her first name is Tanya, but she still can't remember her last name."

Garth nodded in consent and Tanya spoke up. "I don't understand. Why in the world do these people want to hurt the twins and I?"

"It must be something your husband was involved with," Rusty told her; "but until we can find out who he is, or what he was doing, we won't have an answer for you. As far as to why they're coming after the three of you—they probably think you have something they want. We just can't figure out what. The search of your possessions turned up nothing."

"You're probably right about that," Jake added. "I'm sure we'll know soon enough."

After dinner, they all cleaned the kitchen and finished up a few other chores. Much to the twins' dismay, Rusty and Tanya put them to bed. It had been a big day and they were still too excited to sleep. "I think I'll read them a story to help them settle down," Tanya said. "Then I'll go off to bed. I'm feeling a bit pooped myself."

"Good night then," Rusty said. "If you have any problems from that bump on your head, come wake me immediately."

"I will," she promised. "Thanks for all you've done, I appreciate it." Then standing up on tiptoe, she gave him a kiss on the cheek.

Holding her a moment longer, he said, "My pleasure, ma'am. You get a good night's sleep and I'll see you in the morning. Good night, girls."

"G'nite, Daddy," they both chimed.

40

About one o'clock in the morning, Rusty heard the pitter-patter of tiny feet. Then the twins were climbing into his bed, one on each side of him.

"We heard a noise and thought you might be lonely and scared," Stacy said.

Rusty grinned. "Well, I most certainly am, come give me a cuddle."

The twins laughed with him and snuggled up to him. Soon they were all fast asleep.

At about three o'clock, Tanya burst into the room hysterically. "The twins are missing," she screamed. "I couldn't sleep and went in to check on them and they were gone!"

Reacting on instinct, Rusty began reaching for his 9mm when suddenly he heard a whimper and remembered that they were with him and turned on the light instead. Tanya breathed a huge sigh of relief when she saw the girls were there with him.

"We thought Daddy might be a little lonely and scared, so we decided to keep him company," Tracy told her mother. "We didn't mean to scare you, Mommy."

Tanya had to laugh at the picture her daughter was painting of Rusty. "Well, I'm a little lonely and scared too. Does anyone mind if I join you too?"

"Not at all." Rusty moved closer to the edge of the bed and moved Tracy to the center with Stacy. Tanya then crawled in on the other side of the bed.

"You just stay on your side of the bed, Mr. Kincade," she said sternly.

"You're just tryin' to ruin all my fun, aren't ya," he complained in fun.

Blushing, Tanya continued, "I happen to be a married lady—I think. I can't seem to remember too much yet."

"Your honor is safe with me, ma'am," he reassured her with the best half bow he could manage under the circumstances. Then he turned out the light. Lying there, Rusty couldn't help but remember the kiss she'd given him earlier and how nice she'd felt against him. Knowing she was in his bed, but unattainable was heavenly torture. *As hard as it may prove to be, I have to keep taking this slowly—but I will have her eventually.* With that last thought, he drifted off to sleep.

On the other side of the bed, Tanya was having her own thoughts on the subject. *How can I be so attracted to this man? I feel as if we belong together, but I'm married, or at least very recently widowed. I shouldn't be having these kinds of feelings yet. What about the twins? I know I must be their mother, I remember taking care of them and having them around—but I don't remember having them. When were they born? I guess it will come back to me eventually.* With that last thought, she also drifted off to sleep.

41

The next morning, at around six o'clock, Rusty got the twins up quietly, being careful not to wake up Tanya. "Go get ready for your morning exercises," he whispered to them. They hurried off to their room.

Geri had the twins working out to aerobic tapes each morning while the adults worked out with the cardio and weight machines. They loved every minute of it and were doing well with them. Rusty was proud of them and enjoyed watching them. They were both quick learners and since they were young, they were very agile.

Tanya woke up at about eight o'clock and noticed that everybody was gone. She hurriedly went to her room, cleaned up, got dressed and went to find out where everyone was. As she was walking toward the living room, she heard a commotion coming from down a hall she hadn't been down yet. Heading in that direction, she found the workout room and walked in.

Rusty saw her the second she entered the room. "Hi there. The twins and I decided to let you sleep. You had a hectic day yesterday."

"Thank you." She found a chair and sat down to watch the twins going through their exercise routine. She couldn't believe how well they were doing.

Seeing her watching, Geri called over, "If you want to join us tomorrow morning, you're more than welcome to." Relishing the idea, Tanya smiled and nodded.

Tracy piped up. "Hi, Mommy. Wasn't sleeping in Daddy's bed fun?"

The whole room went silent for about ten seconds, then everyone burst out laughing, except Tanya who was turning about ten shades of red, each one darker than the last. Jake was laughing so hard, he had to go to his knees and hold onto one of the weight benches. Rusty went over to Tanya, who was almost in tears. "It's okay. They don't mean anything by it."

Stacy went over to where Jake was bent over the weight bench. She was now head high with him. She cocked her little head sideways and looked him straight in the eyes and said, "You got a problem, Cowboy?" That did it. Jake fell to the floor, laughing harder than ever.

Tracy joined Stacy, staring down at Jake. "My mommy can sleep in my daddy's bed anytime she wants to!" she stated firmly. Then everyone else in the room started laughing again, including Tanya.

Garth was ready to make a cute comment, but Sandy caught him and gave him the look that said, "If you do, you're dead meat." She then spoke up, looking at both Garth and Jake. "One more word from either one of you, and I'll slap both of you silly."

Realizing that she could probably follow through on that threat in their weakened state, they both motioned pulling a zipper across their mouths. At that, both twins started laughing.

"Okay, enough on the subject," Geri interjected into the melee. "It's just about time for everyone to get cleaned up and get ready for breakfast."

"Sounds good to me," Tanya said. "Why don't I get the girls cleaned up? We'll meet you in the kitchen."

"Out of the mouths of babes," Garth murmured to Jake as they left the room and they both started to laugh again as they headed down the hall.

42

Ten minutes later, Rusty had finished enjoying a steaming hot shower. He was half-dressed when he heard Tanya calling for him. Dropping what he was doing, he hurried from his room. *I hope the twins aren't giving her any trouble.* As he entered the girls' room, he blurted, "Is everything okay? What's wrong?"

Tanya looked up at him. She couldn't believe the size of his massive chest and arms. *That is one big hunk of a man,* she thought, then she noticed the big scar on his right side going almost to his heart. Forcing her eyes up from his chest to meet his eyes, she said, "Everything's okay. I just wanted to ask you about earlier." Rusty relaxed and sat down in the reading chair next to the beds. Tanya continued, "Do you think they all took the episode in the weight room the wrong way. I was really embarrassed."

"Don't worry about that. It gave everyone the opportunity to release a lot of tension that has built up around here the past few months." Spotting the twins eavesdropping around the doorway, he grinned at them and motioned them in.

Oblivious to the twins coming in, Tanya asked, "How did you get that nasty looking scar?"

"We want to know too," chimed in Stacy. Tanya jumped at the sound of her voice.

"What are you doing, sneaking up on me like that?" she asked playfully as she pulled a giggling Stacy into her lap. "You're all wet! What are you two doing out of the tub already? If you're big enough to get out of the tub by yourselves, you're big enough to scoot back in there and get yourselves dried off and dressed."

"Make it quick," Rusty called after them as they took off.

"Breakfast should be just about ready." Laughing, he returned his attention to Tanya. "Do you want a nice story or the truth?"

"I'd really like to know what happened."

"If I tell you the truth, it has to remain here. No one outside of who's on this ranch now needs to know."

"That's fine. It looks like you came out second best with that battle. What happened?"

"Well, that depends on what you call second best. Do you remember the big guy with the large scar down the left side of his face? It probably goes all the way to his jugular vein."

"The one that hit me over the head?" she asked warily.

"That's the one. He happens to be a very deadly foreign agent. He is very good at what he does and doesn't care about innocents that get in his way. You and the wins are very lucky to still be alive." Then, leaving out his own identity and any facts about Sonya, he told her about the fight with Black Raven in Poland.

When finished, he said, "I'll fill in other details later, when the time is right. In the meantime, don't discuss this with anyone else. They won't give you any other information anyhow, but I don't want them feeling any more pressure than they do now."

Putting her hand on the scar, Tanya promised to keep the conversation under wraps. Rusty loved the feeling of her hand on his chest, and started to pull her into him, but then the twins walked in chattering.

Tanya pulled away and smiled at him. "Thank you for taking me into your confidence. I'll take the girls with me. Why don't you finish getting dressed, and we'll see you in the kitchen for breakfast." She then herded the twins out toward the kitchen.

43

By eight-thirty, everyone was sitting down to a hot breakfast of French toast and sausage. There was more laughter and a lot less tension than usual. *It's good to see everyone relaxed,* Rusty thought as he looked around. *Tanya looks like she is starting to feel like less of an outsider and more a part of the team. That's good. I just hope everyone doesn't get too complacent, we'll probably see a lot more trouble before this mystery is solved.*

After breakfast the three women and the twins started clearing the table and getting the dishes done. The men went outside to the front porch. "You look like a guy falling hard," Garth said to Rusty, once they were out of earshot of the women. "That Tanya's a lovely lady."

After weighing it in his mind, Rusty said, "You might be right. Just one thing though, I don't think I will ever get over Sonya."

"You never will," Garth said. "I had a similar experience, but my first real love was killed in a car accident."

"You've never mentioned that. I can't imagine you with anyone but Sandy."

"My love for Sandy is very deep, but memories of my first love will never completely leave me."

Jake joined the conversation, "That Tanya is one beautiful and smart young filly, and even though she ain't Sonya. I'm sure she'd like to fill that void you keep talkin' about."

Rusty thought about all this for a couple of minutes. "You two are probably right, but I need to take this slow. I don't want to put the three of them in any more danger than they're in right now."

"I don't think they can be in any more danger than they already are," Garth said. "You just need to stay aware of everything going on around them."

"Speakin' of danger," Jake added, "I'd just as soon not have Geri know anythin' about the Iceman or the Black Raven. You know, we've got to take them both out for good, if any of us is ever gonna sleep better. She wouldn't understand what needs to be done about scumbags." Rusty and Garth both nodded their agreement.

"I don't think they're going to risk their necks until they think they've located whatever it is they've come for," Garth said. "We may have a long wait, since so far none of us have any answers and don't know what it is they want."

"I'm sure the key is locked in Tanya's mind somewhere," Rusty added. "Maybe when we figure out who her husband was, we'll be able to make the connections we need."

"Why not try some of that truth serum?" asked Jake.

"With her head injuries, we can't risk it right now," answered Rusty. "We just might lose her forever."

"And I think Rusty likes her just the way she is," Garth added, chuckling. "Well, we'll just have to watch her as closely as we do the twins."

Wrapping it up, Rusty said, "Garth, go ahead and fill Sandy in on all this, so she can stay up to date on everything. The others should stay in the dark until this is all over. We don't want to give them any more cause for worry than they have already."

44

The women and the twins came out to join the men on the porch. Sandy and Geri sat down next to Garth and Jake. Tanya had the twins pulling her by the hand towards the porch stairs.

"The girls are going to show me the tree house," Tanya called over her shoulder.

"She can't remember it, Daddy," Tracy said, as she and Stacy dragged their mother down the stairs.

"Well, have fun," Rusty called after them, laughing. It was good to see them together like that.

They were about halfway to the tree house, when the alarm suddenly went off. Geri was up like a flash, running after them. Catching up, she grabbed up Stacy. "Get Tracy!" she told Tanya. "Then run to the tree house." Tanya instantly complied.

The rest of the group had gone back into the house and were grabbing the headsets that could be monitored from the tree house. As soon as Geri had turned on the monitor, Rusty said, "Sandy and Garth will be the gold team, Jake and I will be the red team. Good luck, everyone."

With that, Sandy and Garth headed toward the left side of the property; Jake and Rusty took the right side. "There are about twelve bogies coming down the path."

That doesn't make sense, Rusty thought, *Why would they come straight down the path?* "Everyone approach the path carefully," he said, "but hold your fire."

They crept up to the edge of the path, and there were about a dozen teenagers strolling noisily down the path. The four of them came out with weapons drawn and blocked the path.

"This here is private property," Jake called out. "What the hell are y'all doin' here?"

The teens stopped and started muttering among themselves nervously. Finally one of them stepped up as spokesman. "We saw a lake down there and just wanted to go swimming. We didn't mean any harm."

Motioning for the others to put their weapons away, Rusty stepped forward. "If you want to swim in the lake, you need to let me know in advance. If nothing is going on, I'll let you in for a couple of hours, but right now is not a good time."

"We're sorry, Mister. Thanks for understanding, and we'll sure take you up on that invite later."

Reaching into his pocket for a pen and paper, Rusty continued, "The name's Rusty, and here's my number. Call first, and if it's safe, I'll have someone at the gate to let you in. But no more than the number you have here now. Okay?"

"Okay."

The four of them escorted the kids back to the gate. They were much quieter on the way out to the gate than they had been coming in. Once the gate was opened, they ran through it with relief, with just a few covert glances back. Once they made it to the main road, they started chattering again excitedly.

"I doubt that bunch will be back," Jake said with a grin. "I think we scared the hell out of them."

"I think you may be right," Rusty agreed grinning back. Then to Geri he said, "All clear. Everything's back to normal."

"Thank heaven," they heard her exclaim as they headed back to the house.

Back in the tree house, Geri started explaining to Tanya all that had happened.

"Well, I sure feel a lot safer with such an elaborate security system," Tanya said.

"It's state of the art," Geri told her. Then she headed down out of the tree house in order to give the twins and their mother, a little time to themselves.

45

Upon reaching the ground, Geri saw Jake headed for the tree house. She ran to him and gave him a big hug.

"I sure am glad that it turned out to be a bunch of teenagers instead of a real problem."

Jake grinned down at her. "What? A fella can't have a little fun now and then?"

Rusty joined them. "Is this gentleman harassing you again, ma'am?"

"Well, I guess I wouldn't exactly call it harassment."

Rusty smiled. "You must kinda like that old Texan a little bit then," he said teasing her.

"He is kinda cute—in a funny sort of way," she responded. Then smiling, she decided to return the jab. "I'd have to say that you seem to have the same kinda problem where Tanya's concerned."

Everyone laughed and Rusty's face turned a slight shade of red. "I reckon you just might be right about that," he admitted.

"She's a great gal, and I really like her," Geri said, as she smiled up at him. "I don't think you could do much better."

"Well, I'll have to take it slow. I'm just worried about the twins. I don't want her to want me just for their sake. Eventually, she's going to want to take them home, and I'll have to give them up."

"I don't think I'd worry about that too much," Geri reassured him. "She strikes me as a person that makes her decisions honestly."

"The other problem," Rusty continued worriedly, "is that we don't know for sure that her husband is dead. Once we know that, I might get a clean shot; until then though, we have to play it straight."

Garth cut into the conversation. "Remember, the Raven told them he had killed him."

"Yeah, but that could have just been to scare them in order to get them to cooperate. I'll just have to wait and see."

"Jake, Krista is waiting for me," Geri said.

"That's right! I'm going to drop off Geri to visit her sister-in-law for the evening," Jake said, checking his watch. "I should be back shortly."

At that moment Tanya and the twins emerged from the tree house.

Smiling, Rusty said, "I think I'll take them to the lake for a while. See you guys later." With that, he walked over to meet them as they reached the bottom rung of the ladder. Holding up a hand to help Tanya down to the ground, he asked her, "Would you like to see the lake now?"

The twins jumped down and excitedly encouraged their mother to say yes.

"Well, I guess that decides it," she laughed. "Lead on."

The four of them joined hands and headed down the path toward the lake. As they strolled along, Rusty submerged himself in the moment. It was about seventy-five degrees cool in the forest and he enjoyed the musty smell of the redwoods and the different songs of the many small birds. Up on a tree branch ahead, he spotted a stellar jay and pointed it out to the others.

"It's just beautiful here, Rusty," Tanya said quietly, not wanting to startle anything that might be around.

"You should see it early in the morning with the mist coming off the lake. It's downright magical sometimes."

"Are there any fish in the lake?"

"There's lots of fish, Mommy," Stacy answered. "Garth took us here lots of times when he went fishing."

When they reached the lake, Rusty went to the boat dock shed and brought out three fishing poles, a tackle box and a pail of bait. As he handed the two smallest rods to the girls, their eyes lit up.

"Do we get to fish today, Daddy?" Tracy asked excitedly.

"You've got it."

Then Rusty handed Tanya the third rod, which she took eagerly. Showing her experience, she had the hook baited and in the water within a minute. Then she helped Rusty get the twins' rods ready with bobbers and worms. When they were ready, they each helped one of the twins cast the line into the water. They didn't do too badly for their second time out.

Ten minutes had gone by without a bite, and the twins were starting to squirm.

"Aren't they going to bite, Daddy?" Stacy asked.

"You know you just have to be patient, Honey. Fishing can take a long time."

Suddenly Tracy's bobber went down. She had been watching it so intensely that she almost fell in the water when it did.

"Hold on, Sweetheart, I'm coming," Rusty told her as he jogged over to the spot she had picked out.

As he reached her, the bobber went down more sharply, Rusty jerked the line to set the hook and the fight was on.

Tracy was yelling and screaming, "Get it, Daddy! Get it!" over and over again.

"Settle down, Tracy! I'll help you reel him in, but it's your fish, you 'get it,' okay?"

By this time Jake and Garth arrived, having run like hell to see what the screaming was all about. Tracy was reeling in her line as best she could, with Rusty standing ready, just in case she needed help. As the fish reached the dock, he grabbed the net to scoop up the fish.

Suddenly, Stacy's bobber went down and she started jumping and screaming excitedly too. Garth had to grab her before she went tumbling into the water. Then he started helping her bring her fish in, too.

Meanwhile, Rusty had Tracy's fish in the net and had brought it up to the dock for her to see. It was a catfish, weighing a little over a pound.

"It sure is ugly, eeyukie," she said when she saw it.

"It might be ugly, but it sure is good eating," Rusty reassured her as he handed the net to Garth so he could bring in the bass Stacy had hooked.

By now, Tanya had a trout and was bringing it in like a pro, Jake pulled out the instamatic he had in his shirt pocket and starting taking pictures of the event. When he was done and all the fish had been de-hooked and put in the bucket, the twins were too excited to sit through more fishing, so they put everything away and went back up to the house.

46

Back at the house, Jake and Rusty made quick work of cleaning the fish so Sandy could fry them up. Jake could see that Rusty had a lot on his mind, so they worked in silence, allowing him to work it all through.

Rusty had never seen the twins so excited, and knew they were hooked for life. That was especially nice, since obviously, Tanya also enjoyed fishing. *I'm really falling for her hard, I have got to find out who she is and whether or not her husband is still alive before we both get hurt. He probably isn't, the Raven doesn't tend to lie about things like that, but we've got to make sure. It's interesting . . . she's like Sonya in quite a few ways, but loving her is so different from loving Sonya. Just as intense, but different. I really think I could spend the rest of my life with her.*

Just then the twins came bursting in. "Can we go fishing again tomorrow, Daddy?" Tracy asked.

"We'll have to wait and see; but we'll try to go fishing at least two or three times a week. Okay?"

"If for some reason your dad can't take you, Garth or I will," Jake told them, laughing.

"Now, let's take these fish into the kitchen so they can get cooked," Rusty said and he and the twins headed for the kitchen with their catch. Jake stayed behind to clean up the sink.

Thirty minutes later, everyone sat down to enjoy the fried fish, french fries and green salad Sandy had made. The twins were starting to wind down and looked tired, so when they finished dinner, Tanya took them in for their bath and to get ready for bed.

Once she had left the room, Garth quietly said, "I think Tanya has got it bad for you."

"I know she does," Sandy added. "She's a real sweetheart. Don't let this one get away, Rusty."

"It sure wouldn't hurt my feelings any if it's true," Rusty said, "but we don't know for sure if she is free to get serious about anyone."

Garth scoffed at that. "If he was still alive, he would have already tried to locate her and the kids. Besides, you know the Black Raven doesn't lie about his conquests. Even if it was a mistake, and he wasn't trying to kill him, he would turn it into a conquest instead of admitting to a mistake."

"That makes sense to me," Jake added. "It sure would be nice to know what the guy did for a living though, to have Raven go after him like that. We also don't know why he killed Sonya, but I'm sure it all must fit together somehow."

"That may be possible, but I don't see the connection. We may be trying to find one solution to fit all of our mysteries, and that may not be the case. There may be no relationship at all. Only time will unravel this mess."

With that, they all got up and started clearing the table. Garth stayed in the kitchen to help Sandy clean up, Jake went outside to take a tour around the property, and Rusty went in to give the twins a good night kiss and listen to their prayers.

As he was tucking them in, Tracy sat back up and looked up at him. "Do you really like our mom?"

"What do you mean by that? Of course I like your mom."

"But is she your girlfriend?"

Rusty sat down on the bed and gave her a big hug. "We'll just have to wait and see what happens. Okay?"

"Okay," she said as she snuggled happily in his arms.

"Good night, girls. I love you."

"I love you too, Daddy," they both chorused. After their big day, they would soon be sound asleep. He turned out the light, closed the door to a crack and went back out to the living room.

195

47

When Rusty came into the living room, everyone was gathered around the television watching a movie. He saw that there was a vacant spot next to Tanya, and headed over to claim it. He casually put his arm on the back of the couch behind her and she leaned into him. He dropped his arm to her shoulder and enjoyed feeling her warmth against his chest. He knew damn well that the others were getting a kick out of watching them, but he didn't mind, he just wanted her as close as possible. *I wish we were alone right now. We could be having a cozy night by the fire just enjoying each other. Well, maybe someday.*

After the movie was over, everyone retreated toward his or her own bedrooms. Rusty walked Tanya to hers and bent over to kiss her gently goodnight. She responded warmly.

"I had a wonderful day being with you," he said.

She squeezed his hand. "Thank you. The day was perfect for me too." Then she slowly closed the door and Rusty headed for his own room with the memory of that loving kiss they had shared.

Unable to go to sleep just yet, he decided to take a hot shower. It would feel good and probably relax him. His mind kept bouncing back and forth between enjoying his time with the twins and the wonderful kiss from Tanya.

Lying in bed after his shower, he was happy and content for the first time since hearing the news about Sonya. *But I can't let my guard down. The Raven and the Iceman are still out there somewhere just waiting for an opportunity to strike.* He was just about to fall asleep, when he heard his door open slowly. Looking toward it, he saw Tanya's silhouette in his doorway. She was radi-

196

antly beautiful and took his breath away. Frozen for a moment at the sight, he then came to his senses and invited her in.

As she walked into the room, he moved over in the bed and turned back the blanket for her to join him. They spent the next two hours loving and talking and confirming their love to each other. Then they fell into a sound sleep in each other's arms.

Around four in the morning, Tanya woke up, gave Rusty a kiss on his forehead and got out of bed. Rusty pulled her back down playfully.

"Where are you going," he growled and started kissing her.

Laughing softly, she managed to extract herself. "I don't want to go through another embarrassing moment like the other morning."

"Don't worry about them. I love you, that's all that matters."

"I know. I love you too and hopefully we can have more wonderful nights like last night, but I've got to go back to my room."

Rusty let her go, and she glided out. Rusty lay back and enjoyed the lingering sensation of her kiss as he drifted back to sleep.

Part XII

Answers and Retribution

48

The next few weeks passed them quietly into October and the love between Rusty and Tanya grew. The twins noticed how close they were becoming and relished the idea that they might get married, but managed to keep those hopes to themselves, so as not to ruin anything.

Then one morning the adults were finishing their morning coffee and Tracy ran into the room with Stacy close at her heels.

"Look what we found, Mommy! It's your Bible!" Tracy said excitedly.

"We found it under our bed when we were lookin' for Raggedy Ann!"

Tanya took the Bible from Tracy. It was a small white book with a zipper closure. Rusty looked at her quizzically.

"Have you had that with you this whole time, Sweetheart?"

"Probably," she answered hesitantly. "I would never part with it; my husband gave it to me. I must have lost it when I was Rose." She stopped for a moment and smiled. "I just remembered his name! Seeing this Bible has triggered that memory. His name is Don Lewis." She started to blush as she started to feel guilty about the relationship she'd been sharing with Rusty the past few weeks.

Rusty could sense her discomfort and held her hand in comfort. "Do you remember what he did for a living?"

She shook her head.

"Do you mind if I look at the Bible?"

She handed it over to him. "Do you think it can be of help?"

"Maybe." Rusty handed the book to Garth. "You're the expert. See if you can find anything in here that can tell us anything about what her husband was or what he may have been working on. He may have hidden something in it." Garth took the book and headed to his cabin in order to study it without any distractions.

"Jake, get Smokey on the phone and give him Tanya's husband's name. Ask him to get back to us as soon as possible with any information he can get on it." Jake nodded and headed into the living room.

The twins were squirming in excitement, trying not to interrupt. Rusty motioned them over to him and gave them each a big hug. "You two did great!" Then he took the three of them down to the rec room in order to keep them busy while he waited for an update from either Smokey or Garth.

49

Jake came down to the rec room after talking to Smokey. "He says he'll call as soon as he has something for you. We should have something soon."

Rusty looked at Tanya to see how she was holding up. "We may be finding out some things that you'll find difficult to handle. Will you be ready?"

"I honestly don't believe Don is alive," Tanya reassured him. "Between that and everything else that has been going on lately, I should be able to handle anything else that comes along."

"I know it's not right," he said, "but if it turns out you're wrong and he is alive somewhere, I know I'm going to lose the best thing in my life right now."

He could see the tears starting to well up in her eyes.

"Oh, Rusty, I know that even if he's alive, no matter what, I love you. Don was a good man and took great care of the twins and I, but our love was never as deep as the love I share with you; we'll work it out somehow. Besides, if he *is* alive, why would this guardian angel you and the twins talk about have given them to you as your daughters?"

"Do you always know how to make it all sound sensible?" he asked, wanting to accept any straw of logic that might make everything work out the way he wanted, but pragmatism got the better of him.

"Whenever possible."

"We'll just have to wait and see how it turns out. Whatever decision is made will have to be made by you. I won't pressure you either way."

Seeing their mother was upset, Stacy came over to see what was wrong.

"Are you okay, Mommy? Why are you cryin'?"

"Oh, honey, Mommy's just a little sad. It's okay. Do you think I could get a hug?" She leaned down and hugged Stacy. "Now, go on back and play your game."

"Do you want to play Chutes & Ladders with us?"

"Not right now, sweetie, maybe later."

Stacy went back to join her sister at the game table.

Just then, Geri came into the room and immediately noticed the tension. "I'm back and I have cookies! Does anybody want a sugar cookie?"

"I do!"

"I do!"

Both twins came running over to her to get their cookies and to welcome her back.

"Where've you been, Geri?" Tracy asked.

"Don't you remember? I went to visit my sister-in-law. She's living at my house while I'm living here. That way she can take care of my cat and plants while I'm gone."

"Oh yeah, I forgot."

"Can we do our aerobics now?" Stacy asked.

"Let's wait 'til tomorrow morning. Okay? It's kind of late in the day for that," Geri replied. "How about if instead, we go upstairs to the kitchen and fix up some hot chocolate to go with those cookies?"

She then waved to the others and escorted the twins upstairs so that the adults could talk more freely. Rusty nodded his thanks.

"Let's go for a walk," he suggested. He and Tanya headed upstairs and out the front door.

50

It was a cool sixty-five degrees outside and the sun was close to setting for the night. Holding each other close for warmth, they headed toward the lake. The birds were oddly quiet. Arriving at the lake, they sat on the dock, legs dangling over the water. Suddenly they felt a low rumble and the dock moved briefly beneath them. Tanya grabbed Rusty in fear, eyes wide.

"It's okay, sweetheart," Rusty said gently. "It was just an earthquake. It's stopped now, so wipe that fright from your eyes and let's go check on the children."

"I love you so much."

"I love you so much, too."

They headed back to the house, arriving just as the girls and Geri poured out of the house to come looking for them.

"Did you feel that, Mama?" asked Tracy excitedly.

"It was a earthcake!" Stacy added. "The whole house was shakin' and the flower vase fell over!"

"Yes, I did," Tanya said, laughing. "That was quite some earthquake."

"Jake is checking the news to see how strong it was and where it was centered," Geri told them. "Garth and Sandy went down to the gate to make sure the security system wasn't damaged."

"Well, it sounds like everything is well in hand," Rusty said. "I think I'll join Jake and get some more info on it. Did you want to come, Tanya?"

"No, I think I'll stay with the girls for a while. We'll see you later."

"They say it was a 5.2 earthquake, centered north of Point

Reyes," Jake said as Rusty joined him in the living room. "It does-n't look like there was too much damage so far. Just some stuff falling off shelves in the stores and stuff."

Rusty was about to sit down when the phone rang. Jake an-swered it and then handed it to Rusty.

"It's Smokey. Says he needs to talk to you privately. I'll go check on Geri and the girls."

Privately? That's a first. He must have found out something crucial. "Hey, Smokey, why the secrecy?"

"Some of my news pertains to just you, you can share the rest with the others later. To start with, Tanya's husband was working on a project creating a substance that would work better than metal in outer space, but he died from a heart attack before he could turn it over to the organization."

"Are you sure it was a heart attack of natural causes? A lot of my own enemies have died of 'heart attacks' over the years."

"This is true, but he did have a bad heart, so we just assumed it was a natural one. We believe he was finished with the formula, but that he was suspicious of something and so hid it somewhere. The thing that has kept us from identifying him as Tanya's hus-band is that we have no record of them having any children."

"Well someone must have blown that assignment," Rusty said. "The girls certainly know who their mother is."

Jake burst into the room suddenly and Rusty put his hand over the mouthpiece of the receiver. "Garth says he's found some-thing in that Bible of Tanya's! He says it looks like some kind of formula, but he can't figure out what it would be for. Considering how much he likes to tinker around with things, it must be a hell of a formula for him to not be able to figure it out."

"It seems Garth has found a gem of lost knowledge in the Bi-ble he's been reading," Rusty said to Smokey, dropping into code, just in case the line had been tapped again. "We'll have to let him share it with you sometime. Thanks for your information and we'll let you know if we find out anything."

After hanging up the phone, he went into the kitchen, Jake, Geri, and Tanya were still sitting around the table enjoying warm cups of coffee.

Looking at Jake as he walked in, he said, "Can you get everyone else in here for a quick meeting?" Then sitting down next to Tanya, he turned his chair to face her and took both of her hands in his. "Sweetheart?"

Tanya looked at him anxiously. "What's wrong?" she asked anxiously.

"I just got a call confirming the Raven's claim. Your husband died of a heart attack last spring. Whether of natural or suspicious means isn't clear."

Tanya gasped; her face turned white, she broke out in a cold sweat and started shivering. Rusty pulled her over onto his lap and held her close, trying to warm her up. Jake came in and after taking in the situation he went over to Geri to find out what was going on.

Tanya stopped shivering and was feeling calmer in a few minutes. She sat up, but didn't move back to her chair. "I'm sorry. I knew it was true in my head, but I guess my heart still believed he was alive out there somewhere. He was such a good and generous man."

The twins arrived with Garth and Sandy. Seeing their mother on Rusty's lap, they ran over. "Why are you in Daddy's lap, Mommy?"

"Oh, I'm just being a silly goose," she said to them smiling. Turning back to Rusty she said, "I think I'll take the girls for a walk. Okay?"

Rusty gave her one last hug as she got off his lap; she reached for the twins' hands and they left the room.

"Can you follow them, Geri? I'm worried about her, but I can't go right now. We need to have a quick meeting. I'll fill you in on anything you need to know later."

Geri nodded and left the room. Garth and Sandy looked puzzled as they each took a chair.

Rusty started to fill everyone in on his conversation with Smokey. "It turns out that Tanya's husband is that scientist that died of a heart attack last spring. For some reason yet to be determined, Smokey didn't know that he and Tanya had any kids, and he seemed to have died from natural causes, so we had dismissed that possibility earlier.

"Apparently he was working on a formula for a substance that would work better than metal out in space but died before he could turn it over. We need to get the formula from the Bible to Smokey, ASAP.

"Jake, when we're through here, give Sgt. Hagg a call and ask him to provide a private escort for us at about three o'clock this afternoon." Rusty looked at his watch. "That will give us almost an hour to get ready. We'll have him and another officer in the lead car. Garth and Sandy will take the formula and Jake's Lincoln. The formula should be in a secured pouch strapped to Garth's waist. There should be a third car with two more trusted CHP officers following the Lincoln. Jake and I will bring up the rear in my truck. We will follow a little further back as if no part of the group.

"There have been a lot of dead operatives—not to mention the innocent bystanders—in this process of obtaining Don Lewis's formula. I don't want any mistakes on this one. Does anyone have anything else to add?"

No one spoke up. "Then let's get busy. It could be a long day."

Everyone dispersed and Rusty went in search of Geri. Finding her on the front porch watching Tanya and the twins, he pulled a leather pouch out of his back pocket and sat down next to her.

"Garth, Sandy, Jake, and I need to take care of some things. We'll be leaving in a little bit. I'm leaving you in charge of the ranch security. Keep Tanya and the twins with you in the tree house until we return. If we don't return, I need you to get this pouch to Smokey. His phone number is in the envelope in the outside pocket. Take the pouch and hide it in the hidden cupboard in the tree house. It is just inside the door, behind the sign the kids made up. There is a flat button that you push to open it right in the frame of the door next to the sign. Don't turn this over to anyone until you've seen their credentials." Pausing for a moment, he reached into his inside jacket pocket. "Take a look at mine so you know what they should look like. This is very important, so be sure you understand everything before we go. I know you can handle it."

"How dangerous is it going to be for the rest of you?" she asked.

"Don't worry about that. We're all professionals and have been well trained for what we're going to be up against."

"I won't be able to not worry while you're gone. Take good care of Jake for me, okay?"

"It's a deal, I'll take care of Jake, you take care of Tanya and the twins."

"You know I will," she answered.

Just then the twins came running up onto the porch with Tanya walking more slowly behind them.

"Two chip cars, Daddy!"

Rusty looked down the driveway and saw that the CHP cars had arrived.

"Okay, you four; it's time to go to the tree house for a while. I have to go, but I'll see you all later."

He helped them all up the tree and strolled over toward Jake and Sgt. Hagg. Jake was filling him in on what needed to be done.

"We really appreciate your assistance in this," Jake was saying as Rusty approached.

"I'm enjoying all the excitement. We don't usually get to see much action in this part of the state," the Sergeant said.

"Are we ready?" Rusty asked. "Let's get moving. Garth! Sandy!"

Garth and Sandy came out of the house and got into the Lincoln. Sgt. Hagg stopped at the window of one of the CHP cars and told them to follow the Lincoln. Then he headed over to the other CHP car and climbed into the passenger side. The three cars took off heading toward Willits. A few minutes later Jake and Rusty followed, barely keeping them in sight.

51

They had been on the road for about five minutes when Jake said, "We've got company. That little turnout Garth and I used in our last run in is just ahead."

Rusty looked back and saw a blue car about a quarter mile back. "Well, it's not less than we expected. I'll slow down a little, so they'll get a little closer. I'm familiar with that turnout, it should work nicely. I'll stop them there."

Rusty flashed his headlights to the cars ahead, letting them know they would be stopping and to continue on. A couple of minutes later, with the blue car right behind them, Rusty forced the truck to a skidding halt, causing it to make a ninety degree turn. The other car had to turn into the clearing in order to avoid being hit. Rusty backed the truck up into the clearing and stopped about fifty feet from the car. As he stepped out of the truck, he saw the Black Raven and the Iceman emerge from the car and start to head over to the truck.

"As usual, it's a pleasure to see you again? How's the eye?" Sundance asked nonchalantly. He had taken out the Raven's eye in their last encounter, when he had received the injury to his arm.

"Sundance! Long time no see! How's the arm?" the Black Raven responded with an overconfident smile.

"Well, well, well, fahncy meeting ya'll here," Cowboy drawled, with a cocky grin as he stepped out of the truck. "I decided to come along, just in case I was needed to kinda, you know, even up the odds."

Both of the Russian agents stopped their approach when he appeared, obviously surprised to see him.

"You mean you didn't learn anything from our last go round, Cowboy?" the Iceman asked.

"Why, ah'm just gettin' started!"

The four of them sized each other up, knowing that this would be the ultimate and final battle. At least two of them would not be leaving this battleground. Then, as if by some unseen signal, all four swung into action.

Knife in hand, Sundance rushed the Raven, who smartly knocked the knife out of his left hand and left a deep wound on his right arm. Sundance stepped to the Raven's blind side and struck him a massive blow that crushed part of the Raven's skull. The Raven fell back in excruciating pain and Sundance reached over and shot one of his poison darts into the Raven's neck.

"Thanks for the easy out, Sundance," the Raven said as he realized what had been done.

"Don't count on it," Sundance replied. "This is a slower working poison than what I used on the Wasp. You'll have about twenty minutes of pain before you head straight to hell for what you did to Sonya. Why did you kill her?"

The Black Raven remained mute, and Sundance knew he would get no answer.

"These next twenty minutes of pain are for Sonya, Don Lewis, and for the grief you gave to Tanya and the twins."

The Raven tried to move, but his muscles wouldn't respond. The drug had inhibited his muscle control, while allowing him to continue to feel pain that continued to escalate. After seeing the terror and rage in the Raven's eyes, Sundance looked over to see how the Cowboy was faring against the Iceman.

He had just hit the Iceman with a powerful left, and as he went down, the Iceman managed to plunge his knife into the Cowboy's foot. The Cowboy grabbed the Iceman by his hair with one hand to pull his head back, then he sliced his neck across the jugular vein and dropped him back to the ground to let his life's blood soak into the ground.

"Too bad for him he picked the wrong foot," Cowboy laughed. "I didn't feel a thing."

Sundance smiled. "Give me your knife," he said. Then he took the knife over to the Raven and put it into his hand. "Now it looks like they had a duel of their own."

Suddenly, out of the corner of his eye, he saw movement. Out of the dark shadows stepped a menacing figure holding a .45 revolver. It was the head nurse from the hospital that had been so belligerent when the twins had been sick.

"Well, well; what's the head nurse of the hospital doing way out here in the country with a gun, and so obviously in the company of these two thugs?" Sundance asked.

"Why, Sundance! I'm surprised you don't recognize me," she responded.

"Well, I sure do," Cowboy growled. "Sundance, this is the Dark Star."

"Well, I see someone has done his homework," she preened. "I was so disappointed when you didn't know me that night at the hospital, Sundance. I had heard so much about you and thought for sure that you would."

"We've never met before, but I sure had a gut feeling that something was wrong when I got rid of you at the hospital."

"Enough of this small talk," she said suddenly. "Put all your weapons on the ground slowly with two fingers. That German luger that you're so proud of first, Cowboy, then the .38 in your boot. Now you, Sundance, your 9mm, then your dart pistol, and now your knife and the .38 which are strapped to your ankle. I don't want to kill you, I just want the formula. I know about that bad habit you have of making a spare copy of things."

"I'll be damned," he muttered under his breath to the Cowboy, which was their code for him to take the offense as soon as he could. "I guess you've done your homework as well," he said to the Dark Star. "You sure caught us off guard." He reached into his jacket pocket.

213

"Bring it out slowly!" Dark Star demanded.

"Don't give it to her!" Cowboy called out.

"We've run out of options," Sundance told him as he slowly walked over to her to hand her the leather pouch that he had pulled out.

When he was within arm's length, she said, "That's far enough." Then reaching out to grab the pouch, he let it drop to the ground. "That wasn't very smart," she said. "I'm not falling for that old trick. Back away slowly."

She kept her eyes on him until he was far enough back to not interfere with her reaching down to pick up the pouch. Suddenly two gun shots rang out and the Dark Star was dead before she hit the ground, half of her head was blown away.

Sundance looked at the Cowboy incredulously. *What in the hell did you use and how did you keep it so well hidden?*

Cowboy smiled, "I was in Garth's workshop with him when I spotted this weird looking .357 Magnum. It has a flat handle and a new solid cylinder with a spring. It is sort of like a two-shot Derringer. You strap it to your wrist in a special holster, which has a hidden button. When you press the button, the gun pops into your hand and as it does you can get off two quick shots. Dark Star was so intent on watching you, she stopped watching me, so I went for it.

"One problem, though, I think I'll have to have a talk with our boy, Garth. He didn't tell me that he had put in an extra load of gun powder. I don't think my hand is going to stop shaking before we get home and I'm not hearing so well right now."

Sundance laughed. "Well give it to me and I'll put it in the Iceman's hand. I don't feel sorry for the cops on this one. Between a woman with her head blown off, a man with a sliced neck and another man that died from a heart attack, I don't think they will ever unravel this mystery."

Then the two of them cleaned up the rest of the area, leaving

214

no signs that anyone but those three had been there. Then they got back into Rusty's truck and headed back for the Kincade ranch.

"Were you really going to give her that formula?" Jake asked about five minutes later.

"If she had taken that particular formula and mixed up all the ingredients, she would have blown herself up, along with anyone else within a hundred yards of her. I'm almost sorry she didn't get away with it, I can't think of a nicer way to get rid of some very nasty Russian agents."

"You're almost as devious as Garth," Jake said admiringly.

"We come from the same school of thought, only he's a master at it."

"Well, one of these days, I'm going to have to get even with him. That is twice now that he has scared the living daylights out of me."

"It will have to be something extremely good and very underhanded," Rusty warned him. "He doesn't miss too many tricks."

"Oh, it will be. Trust me. By the way, since you didn't have the extra copy of the formula on you, what did you do with it?"

"Don't get mad; but I gave it to Geri to safeguard. She put it in a secret hiding space I told her about in the tree house. I told her that if all else failed, to get hold of Smokey and set up a way for him to get it from her."

"Nah, I'm not mad. She's a brave gal. Besides, the way we built the tree house, it's a virtual fortress. It would take an army to get them out of there. It was a good move. She's proven she's trustworthy and smart. You couldn't have made a wiser choice. They wouldn't expect you to give the only other copy to a non-agent."

Rusty glanced over to Jake to say something more on the subject and caught sight of his foot. "You might want to take that knife out of your foot before Geri sees it and has a fit."

Jake laughed. "I forgot all about it. I still can't believe that the

Iceman either forgot or didn't know about my losing my foot from our last encounter."

"All in all, it's been a pretty productive day," Rusty reflected. "We got rid of three Russian assassins and retribution for Sonya. It does a soul good. Now Sonya, Don Lewis and a few other innocent souls can have closure in their deaths and proceed to the afterlife."

"All we need now is confirmation that Garth and Sandy have delivered the formula without any further problems, and it will make it a perfect day," Cowboy added.

52

Once they were back at the ranch, they were bombarded by hugs and kisses of relief.

"So how did it go?" Geri demanded while checking Jake over front and back to make sure he was all still there.

"There was a little trouble, which we had anticipated," Rusty told them; "but it's all taken care of now, so hopefully, Garth and Sandy will have no problem finishing their part of the mission."

Tanya had been checking Rusty over as closely as Geri was Jake. Finding that his arm was bleeding, she led him into the house so she could take care of it.

"You're going to need some stitches," she said after examining it more closely. Jake arrived with the first aid kit before the words had finished leaving her lips.

Opening it, he pulled out some iodine and a topical numbing agent and applied both to the area of the cut. Rusty hissed at the sting, but soon he stopped feeling any pain in the area. Tanya scooted the twins out of the room while Jake stitched up the gash in Rusty's arm. It required fourteen stitches in all. Then he bandaged it up and gave him a couple of pain killers.

"Take these and call me in the morning," he said grinning.

Rusty chuckled. "Thanks, Dr. Jake. I sure hope you don't intend to bill me for any crooked stitches."

"Well!" Jake said, taking affront. "Try to do a guy a little favor, and listen to him. Humph."

Geri and Tanya walked in at the end of the little by-play and laughed at Jake's expression of indignation.

"The kids are in the kitchen having their supper. What happened out there?"

Taking the initiative, Rusty started relating the events to them.

"To start off with, Geri, don't get mad at us. This was a job that had to be done, just like when you pull someone over for speeding, you just don't know what might happen.

"Tanya, the man that killed your husband, hit you in the head and left you and the twins to die, is now dead. It looks like the drama that we have all been having to endure these past few months is finally at an end, so as soon as we've heard that Garth and Sandy have made their rendezvous with Smokey we can all relax and enjoy life again.

"Garth, Sandy, Jake, and I still have enemies out there, so we can't completely relax our vigil, but living here gives us all a lot more security and allows us to live life at a much less hectic pace."

"Well then, it looks like my job here is over with and I should get back to work," Geri said.

"Actually, if it's alright with you, I'd rather you stayed on a couple more weeks, just in case more trouble develops. I wouldn't want to lose you prematurely. I'll get the approval from Smokey."

Geri's face lit up like the Fourth of July. "I have to admit, it sure will be hard to leave this ranch. I really enjoy its beauty; not to mention its people."

"Well, you can use one of the cottages anytime, and as long as you'd like," Rusty told her. "We enjoy having you here."

Overcome with emotion, Geri went over and gave him a quick kiss and hug. "Oh, thank you so much!" and she ran over to Jake who held her in a big bear hug.

Then Rusty looked at Tanya. "You know I love you and the twins very much."

She nodded shyly.

"I'd like to offer you another one of the cabins while we fig-

218

ure out how we fit together." She gave him a big smile and went over to give him a passionate kiss and hug.

"Wild horses couldn't drag me away," she said as he held her in his arms, and they kissed again, long and hard.

53

A week later, Garth and Sandy arrived back at the ranch. They had decided to take a little vacation while they were in Washington, D.C., and so were in great spirits when they returned.

"Smokey got us tickets to an event being held in honor of the Apollo 8 crew!" Sandy gushed as she got out of the car and started hugging the welcoming committee. "They're set to take off in December to orbit the moon! It's so exciting! We have to be sure to watch it on the television!"

Garth smiled as he joined his wife. "She's been like this for two days. She can't seem to think of anything else. How are things here?"

Rusty started filling him in on what had happened after leaving the ranch. When he got to the part of Jake taking out the Dark Star, Garth interrupted him.

"Were those bullet loads strong enough?" he asked innocently.

Jake grinned. "One of these days I'll get even, just you wait. By the way, if we're done with all of this, Geri and I have an announcement to make. We're getting married next June!"

Everyone started congratulating them all at once.

Once things started to quiet down a little, Rusty spoke up. "Tanya and I are getting married too," he said while watching her face go beet red. "That is if she'll say 'Yes'." He took out an engagement ring he had been carrying around in his pocket and showed it to her. The twins rushed out to find out what all the commotion was about just as Tanya burst into tears.

"Why are you cryin', Mommy?" Tracy asked.

"It's okay, Honey." Then she turned to Rusty and said, "Yes,

yes I'll marry you." Rusty slipped the finger on her finger and held her close.

"Maybe we can make it a double wedding!" Jake said.

"That sounds great to me, if it's alright with the beautiful brides."

Everyone thought it was a great idea.

"What's goin' on, Daddy!" Stacy and Tracy asked in unison.

"I'll take care of this," Tanya said as she led the twins inside where it was quiet and explained everything to them. "Mommy and Daddy are going to get married in June, and so are Jake and Geri. How would you two like to be the flower girls?"

"Ooh, can we really, Mommy?" Stacy asked hugging her while jumping up and down in excitement.

"I wouldn't hear of anything else," Geri said from the doorway.

The girls rushed over to give her a hug too.

Part XIII

Together At Last

54

The next few months passed in a flurry. Richard Nixon was elected President and vowed to reduce tensions between the USA and the USSR; Apollo 8 became the first ship to successfully orbit the moon; and, with Sandy's help, Tanya and Geri excitedly began to put together the details for a beautiful double wedding.

The ceremony was to be held outside, under the big redwoods near the lake. They planned for it to start at 7:00 in the morning, just as the mist began dissipating from the lake, so that the birds could add their music to the ceremony. They wanted the whole thing to appear magical. Their dresses would be white as moonflowers and they would carry flowers and fern that Sandy and the twins would gather the day before.

The reception would be held in the house, as the living room, dining room and rec room were plenty large enough to hold the crowd of guests that were expected to attend.

Jake, Garth, and Rusty spent a lot of time fishing with the twins and working on the construction of the new cabins. Rusty had also ordered four modular houses which arrived in March. One of them was for Jake and Geri and another was for Garth and Sandy. They were his gift to them for their loyalty and for going through some harrowing experiences they hadn't had to. The other two would be used for visitors with families, such as his sister's family and eventually for Judge Hardaway, if he ever decided to move back to the ranch. They were enjoying the fact that they could relax and not worry too much about unexpected surprises.

Rusty was sitting on the porch watching the delivery men set up the modulars. He had been working on his guest list. Smokey and Jim Tate were going to be unable to attend the wedding, due to prior commitments, and felt bad about not being able to take part in the festivities. *I know how hectic their schedules can be, but I wish they could attend anyway. Well, at least I'll see Jim when Tanya and I go to Poland on our honeymoon.*

Jim had made all the arrangements for them as a wedding present. They would be staying in the honeymoon suite with all the trimmings, at the fanciest hotel in town. Jake and Geri had decided upon Hawaii and would be gone a couple of weeks to enjoy the islands, soak in the sun at the beach and just totally relax. Garth and Sandy would take care of the twins while everyone was gone. The four of them were already planning a big fishing trip to Lake Shasta.

Garth and Jake were directing the set up of the homes. They would all be far enough away from each other to insure privacy, but close enough to enjoy each other's company too. It also provided extra security, as the ranch was becoming more and more like a fortress. Rusty had four more security system control panels made up to be placed in each of the houses. If there was any trouble for any of them, the backup wasn't too far away.

It was always in the back of his mind that enemy foreign agents could show up at any time, though that would become less and less likely as time went by. *Some of them will be killed, others will retire and eventually we will be forgotten. But in the meantime, we have to stay prepared.* He thought back to his experience with the Guardian Angel and knew things wouldn't stay quiet for long. *The angel said they would need me until they became of age and six years old is a long way from becoming of age.* While he felt as though a huge load had been taken off his shoulders, at least for the present, he appreciated the fact that his friends would be close by when and if the next emergency arose. *I'll let Tanya enjoy the peace for as long as it lasts. There's no need to worry her, especially before the wedding. I want it to be a day none of us will ever forget.*

The three men were busy over the next few weeks putting in

new porches and decks around the new homes. Both Jake and Garth were in their glory with that assignment. They both loved carpentry work and did a fantastic job. Sandy was kept busy tutoring the twins, helping with wedding plans and creating plans to decorate the house she and Garth would be moving into. The brides-to-be spent their time either fussing over the wedding plans or fussing over decorating their future homes. Tanya had some definite ideas about the main house and wanted to give it a more homey feeling.

"It's beautiful, but it's too much like a bachelor's pad," she explained when Rusty complained that she didn't like what he'd done to the place.

Tanya was also kept busy settling the estate of her late husband. She found out that he had left a hefty life insurance policy to her and the twins. The house they had lived in had been torched, so there was an additional insurance policy to settle. It was decided that the foreign agents burned it down when they didn't find what they were looking for, just to make sure no one else did either. Rusty had hoped there would be more left there for Tanya to explore in the hope that it would help restore her memory. She was still remembering things in piecemeal, but had some big holes left—such as what her husband looked like. Eventually, it should all come back.

55

The day finally arrived for the wedding and the twins were so excited that they could hardly sit still to get dressed for the occasion. It was all Sandy could do to get them in their satin lavender dresses accented with white satin roses before they rushed off to find their mother. Rusty, already in his dark gray tux, intercepted them on the way.

"Whoa there! Where do you little spitfires think you're going?" He grabbed them both up as they squealed in delight.

Sandy came down the hallway. "Don't you look handsome!"

"Ah, I hate these stuffy things," he said as he put the girls down. "They are always choking me." He put his fingers in his collar to demonstrate how tight it was.

"Oh, you'll do fine," she told him. "Now, why don't you take these little hooligans outside so I can go help the brides. It's already six-thirty, the wedding guests will be arriving any minute. Are Garth and Sgt. Hagg at the gate yet?"

"I believe so, but I'll check it out," he said. "Come on, girls, let's go get the flowers out of the cooler and set them up outside."

They headed out to the kitchen to get the flowers.

"Don't take out the bouquets yet!" Sandy called after them as she headed toward Tanya's room where the brides were getting ready for the wedding.

When she entered the room, she saw that both women were already in their dresses and make-up. All that remained were the finishing touches. Geri's sister-in-law was helping her get her veil in place, while Tanya was working with hers in the mirror.

"Let me help you with that," Sandy said as she went over to help Tanya.

228

"Oh, Sandy," Geri exclaimed, "I don't believe you've had a chance to meet my sister-in-law yet. This is Krista. She was married to my older brother, Johnny. He died last year in Vietnam, Krista, this is Garth's wife, Sandy."

"It's very nice to meet you, Krista. I'm so sorry for your loss. Have you been in town long?"

"Thank you. I've been in town for almost a year," Krista said. "I've been house sitting for Geri while she's been here. The change of scenery has been good for me." Then she finished adjusting the veil. "There you go. Perfect? You are just stunning."

Sandy finished with Tanya's veil a minute later and the two brides beamed at each other.

"So, do we have the `something old, something new, something borrowed, something blue' taken care of yet?" Sandy asked as she and Krista got into their maid of honor dresses. They were the same shade of lavender the twins were wearing, but with accents of white lace draped over the lavender satin.

"Well," Geri answered thoughtfully, "the dresses are new, and we each have on blue garters, I have my mother's dress watch on—how about you, Tanya?"

"I'm wearing a gold bracelet I found in Don's safe deposit box, but I haven't done the `something borrowed' yet. Hey, I have an idea. How about if we borrow each other's necklaces? It could add to the connection of the double wedding theme."

"That's a great idea!"

Sandy and Krista helped the two brides exchange their necklaces and readjusted the veils and then they were ready to go.

"I'll go check to see if they're ready for us yet," Sandy said. She left the room to see if everything was ready.

She found Garth on the front porch waiting for her. "Is everything ready?"

"We're ready whenever you are," he reassured her.

"Well then, get everyone in place and I'll go get the bridal party. Where are the twins?"

229

"I'll get them. They'll be here when you get back."

Sandy went back inside to get Tanya, Geri, and Krista. The music started as they approached the designated area with the twins in the lead, scattering flowers on the path. The two grooms were with the minister under the branches of the largest redwood on the property waiting for their brides. Everything proceeded so perfectly it was as if the ceremony was a dream come true.

Afterwards, everyone headed up to the house for the reception. The next few hours were full of champagne and dancing. The day was warming up and Jake came out of the kitchen with a cold white glass in his hand. Garth had been dancing for the last hour and was dripping sweat.

"Hey Garth!" Jake called out. "I know how much you like milkshakes, and you looked so hot I decided to make you one when I made one for the girls."

"Great!" Garth exclaimed and headed over to him. As he handed it over, Jake gave it a little stir and it started to foam up. Garth tilted the glass to take a sip and suddenly he had foam all over his face and hair. He held the glass away from himself with one hand, while he wiped his face with the other. The glass continued to foam away, overflowing onto the floor. Rusty, who had been watching from the kitchen started laughing wildly. Other guests looked over to see what was going on and started chuckling. Soon everyone in the room was laughing, including Garth.

"What the hell was that for?" he demanded. As Sandy and Geri both snapped pictures of the incident. *They'll never let me live this one down,* he thought.

"I told you I'd get even with you," Jake reminded him, laughing even more.

Garth thought back to the grenade incident and the two-shot pistol stunt. "I guess I asked for it," he admitted. "I think you may have souped it up just a little too much though," he added nodding toward the still foaming glass.

"Ah, it's just a little bit of dry ice. I'll go dump it in the sink." Jake took the glass back and headed toward the sink.

The rest of the reception went off without a hitch and soon the guests were leaving and giving their good wishes for happy marriages and fun honeymoons.

56

Rusty and Tanya boarded the plane to Poland at 3:00 that afternoon. It was one of the new 747s that had been introduced that
year. The plane was huge and Rusty couldn't help wondering how
such a large plane could stay up in the air. They had been in the air
for a few hours, when Tanya reached over to grab Rusty's hand.

"I know I have friends and relatives in Poland," Tanya said
worriedly, "but I just can't seem to remember who any of them
are."

"I'm sure that once you get there or see them you'll start to regain your memory about them the way you have about other
things," Rusty reassured her. "I can't wait for you to meet my
friend Jim. He has set everything up for us." He didn't want to tell
her yet that Jim was the American Ambassador to Poland. He
wanted that to be a surprise. "It's been a long time since I've seen
him. Not since right after Sonya was killed."

"Well, any friend of yours is a friend of mine," she told him.

"Thanks," he said, squeezing her hand.

A few hours later the plane landed at its destination. One of
the stewardesses came up to Rusty and Tanya.

"Mr. Kincade? Would you and Mrs. Kincade please follow
me?"

She led them out through a side entrance to the airport and
there stood Jim Tate, looking bigger than life.

He came over to give Rusty a big hug. "Ya look great! So
much betta' than when ah last saw ya!" Then he turned to greet
Rusty's bride and almost fell over backwards in astonishment.
"Tanya! What are you doin' here, gal?"

"Jim, this is my wife, Tanya. Do you already know her?"

Suddenly a flash of realization came over Tanya as she remembered who Jim Tate was. She remembered meeting him at a social function. "Aren't you the Ambassador?" Then her knees started to buckle under her and Rusty caught her and carried her to a nearby bench.

"Are you okay, Sweetheart?"

"I'll be okay. It's just such a shock."

"Will someone please tell me what's going on!" he demanded, looking up at Jim.

Not knowing any way of saying it easy, Jim decided to just tell him outright. "Tanya is Sonya's sistah."

Now Rusty's knees started to go weak and he sat down next to his wife.

"But my sister's name isn't Sonya," Tanya said. "I'm sure of that. That name doesn't ring any bells at all!"

"It wouldn't, Sweetheart," Rusty explained. "It was her code name. We aren't allowed to divulge our true identities while we're working and there's a chance of being forced to divulge information. She only knew me as Sundance and I only knew her as Sonya. We were going to share our true names during our marriage ceremony, once we had both retired."

"Now I remember. You were at the funeral. That's why I thought I'd seen you before."

Jim interrupted. "Tanya was wearin' a black veil and you were so upset ovah the loss of Sonya, you hardly saw anyone there anyway. Then we left early."

Tears started coming from Tanya's eyes and Rusty held her tight. She broke away from him as more memories came flooding back. "I suddenly remembered my husband," she said.

Puzzled, Jim asked, "Just remembered?"

Rusty explained briefly, "The Black Raven killed her husband and hit her over the head with a gun. Then he burned down her home. She's been suffering from amnesia ever since. This meeting seems to be triggering a lot of memories for her."

"Sounds strangah than fiction."

"Life can be that way sometimes," Rusty said. "It certainly has been this past year and a half. That's for sure. First Sonya is killed, then I find the twins wandering around in the cold, then . . ."

"The twins!" Tanya gasped, interrupting Rusty's rhetoric. Then she started crying agin.

This time Jim was the one that knew what was wrong. "Let me explain that one, Tanya." Then he sat down next to Rusty. "You know those twins you found?"

"Yeah. They're Tanya's and Don's daughters."

"Wrong. Those twins belong ta you and Sonya."

"WHAT! That's absurd!"

"Aftah the two of ya got togethah, you had gone to Germany on a mission and she came to me. She was with child. She made me promise not to tell ya, since as long as the two of ya were agents, the child would not be safe. Then she went ta her sistah's place and had the twins. Tanya and Don didn't have any children and agreed to raise them. Sonya said that once you and she were married, she would want the children back, but that they would be able to see them anytime they'd want. She knew that if anyone found out about the twins, their little lives would be wo'thless."

"How come you never told me any of this the last time I saw you?"

"Ya were still an active agent and on a dangerous mission. Ah couldn't allow ya to put them in danger. Betta' that they remained safe with their aunt and uncle. If ah'd known the situation, ah'd have come clean a long time ago."

Rusty stood up and started pacing back and forth. It was a lot to take in at once. *So now, instead of being married to Sonya, I'm married to her sister who has been raising my children for the past six years—well five actually, I've had them for this last year. My children! I can't believe I'm really their father and not just an appointed guardian!*

Suddenly he got a big grin on his face, walked over to his wife and picked her up in a big bear hug. He gave her a big kiss. "Everything will be just fine." Then he set her back down on the bench and sat down between her and Jim and turned to face Jim.

"You and I have been the best of friends for years. Promise me you won't hold out on me like that again."

"Okay, okay, ah promise," Jim said laughing.

"Your punishment is that you are to be Godfather to the twins and if anything happens to me, you will be responsible for making sure they are taken care of."

"But ah don't know anythin' about children! And ah have too many social responsibilities."

"You'll learn, and you'll have to come visit us at the ranch this summer. Get to know the girls. You'll love them."

"Well, ah suppose ah could perhaps manage that," Jim said reluctantly. "But ah don't know anything about little gals."

Tanya reached across her husband's lap and took Jim's hand. "You'll learn," she reassured him.

Jim thought about it for a couple of minutes. 'Y'all may be right. It might be kinda nice. Thanks." He stood up and started pacing back and forth. He started to like the idea. "I want them in Poland each summmah for two weeks. . . ."

"Slow down, old buddy,' Rusty laughed. "Let's take it one step at a time."

Jim started to look indignant but then he started laughing too. "Let's get outa here."

57

When they finally arrived at the hotel, Jim took care of checking them in while Tanya explored the lobby and the gift shop.

"Everything is so beautiful! I just love the idea of having a fountain in the lobby!"

Rusty was enjoying watching his wife delight in the luxuries the hotel offered, when Jim came over with the key to their suite. "Okay, Honey, Jim's got the key. Let's go check out our home for the next two weeks."

Tanya came back to join the men and they all headed over to the elevator with the bell-hop that was handling their bags. They were on the top floor of the hotel and the elevator was mostly glass and traveled the outside wall of the hotel. Tanya started to get dizzy as they approached their floor. She wasn't accustomed to heights. Determined to make the best of it, she stopped watching the ground and turned to face the men.

"The view is gorgeous," she said with a tight smile. She was white as a sheet.

"Are you okay, Sweetheart?" Rusty asked worried. Jim gave him a questioning look with eyebrows raised.

"Oh yes, just a little dizzy, that's all," she answered swaying a little.

Rusty held her close to him until the elevator stopped and they got off. Once they were in the enclosed hallway, Tanya started to feel a little better.

"So, which one is ours?"

"Right down there at the end of the hall."

Jim led the way, opened the double door with a grand gesture and bowed as he motioned them into the room. It was beautiful.

There was a sofa and chair in gold velvet with maroon braid trim and mahogany coffee and end tables and bookshelves. The floor was carpeted in a maroon thick plush that you wanted to just squish your toes into. On one of the bookshelves there was a Marantz stereo system and one of the new Sony Trinitron color television sets that had just come out last year. On the other were a variety of popular books.

At the far end of the room, on a raised platform with a picture window overlooking a park, in front of the window there was a small mahogany dining table with two matching chairs as well as a small refrigerator and host bar in the corner.

Tanya went into the bedroom and gasped. "Rusty, come here!" Rusty joined her in the bedroom and grinned at her astonishment.

The king-size bed was in the center of the room against the far wall. It was covered with a gold velvet bedspread and had lots of pillows. There were two dressers also made of mahogany on either side of the bed. Each of the dressers had a big window above it. The other wall containing the door had a huge, ornate, full length mirror on it. The thick maroon carpet continued throughout the suite.

Tanya sat down on the bed and it sank under her. She gasped again. "It's one of those waterbeds I've heard of! I've never been on a waterbed before!" She lay down on it to get the feel of it. "Oh my goodness! There's a mirror on the ceiling!" She started to blush as she considered the implications of that and Rusty couldn't contain himself anymore. He burst out laughing.

Jim came into the room. "What's goin' on in here?"

"Oh, Tanya's just exploring the bedroom," Rusty said as he got his laughter under control while she gave him a stern look, as if to say, "Don't you dare."

"Well, come look at the bathroom. You'll love it."

They followed him out of the bedroom and into the bathroom. Tanya squealed when she saw the hot tub. The room was done in porcelain white with gold fixtures. There were gold and maroon towels on the walls and gold bath mats next to the tub and sink on the maroon carpet which continued into the bathroom giving it quite a finished and luxurious look.

"Oh, Jim! It's just wonderful!" Tanya gushed. "I've never experienced anything so extravagant and luxurious! How can we ever repay you?"

"Ahem so glad ya like it. Congratulations on your marriage and family. Ahem so happy things have finally turned out well. Now you kids relax and rest up from your flight. I'll see ya for dinner tomorra'."

"Before you go," Rusty stopped him. "I want to visit Sonya's gravesite tomorrow, and I'd like you to be there. Do you think you can get some time away for that?"

"Ah'll see what ah can do. I'll call ya in the mornin'."

Jim left them to enjoy the room and headed back to the Embassy.

"This place is super!" Tanya said. "It must have cost Jim a small fortune!"

"Don't worry about it, Honey," Rusty reassured her. "Knowing Jim, it probably didn't cost him a cent. A lot of people owe him favors. He probably just called some in."

"Well, it was nice of him to spend his favors on us." Tanya looked thoughtful a moment and continued. "You know, you never mentioned anything about anyone in Poland, except Jim, and not much about him. If you had it might have jarred some of my memories back earlier."

"Remember," he reminded her, "there wasn't any reason to believe that telling you about my experiences in Poland might help you. There are lots of things I've done and people I've met in the last fifteen years that I've been an operative. If I'd had any clue that you were related to Sonya, I probably would have talked about Poland more."

238

"This is the most twisted up situation I've ever heard of, much less experienced," she said, shaking her head.

"You can say that again," he agreed, taking her into his arms. "This morning you were the mother and I was the stepfather. This afternoon, I'm the father and you're the stepmother. I'd say that you add a couple of twins to that mix and we've got a pretty neat little family going on. I can't thank you and Don enough for the years you raised them and the love you gave them."

"Don and I knew that when Sonya was ready to take them back, we would be devastated. We both loved the twins very much. I suppose that we should tell the girls the truth about their real mother and father when we get back home."

"I don't think that's necessary right now," Rusty told her. "We can wait until they reach an age and maturity when it will be easier for them to understand. There's no reason to change the fact that you are `Mommy' to them since you will be continuing in that roll."

Tanya reached up and gave him a kiss. "Thank you. I was having trouble getting used the fact that I would become `Aunt Tanya' to them after all these years."

Rusty laughed. "I guess I hadn't thought of that aspect of it yet." Then he changed the subject. "Are you tired? We spent our wedding night on the plane, so we haven't really had one yet. Do you want to try out the hot tub?"

"Mmmm. That sounds wonderful."

239

58

The next morning Jim called and said he would meet them in the lobby at 11:00. Rusty and Tanya were enjoying a hearty breakfast of eggs Benedict and mimosas when Tanya brought up a subject that Rusty knew had been on her mind ever since finding out about his and her sister's relationship.

"Do you think Sonya would approve of us getting married? After all, it seems a little strange that you would fall in love with two sisters, one right after the other."

Rusty got up and went to stand behind her, leaning down to put his arms gently around here. "My love for you is different than my love for Sonya, just as your love for me is different than your love for Don. The fact that you are both sisters (with very different personalities I might add) is pure coincidence. I'm sure fate (or that Guardian Angel of the girls) stepped in and guided the twins to me and then me to you, in order to straighten out this convoluted family in the best way possible after Don and Sonya were lost.

"Sonya loved you enough to entrust her children to you and she loved me enough to want me to be happy if she wasn't going to be here for me. I think she would approve very much that we are all together now."

"Do you always know how to make it all sound sensible?" she asked as she leaned back into him for a hug.

Rusty laughed at having his question thrown back at him. "Whenever possible."

After breakfast they went down to the lobby to meet Jim.

Rusty greeted him with a warm handshake. "The accommodations are just great. I haven't slept so soundly in months."

"Ah'm so glad. Have ya eaten?"

"Oh, yes," Tanya answered. "We just finished a yummy breakfast of eggs Benedict. It was wonderful."

"Well, let's get moving," Rusty said. "It should take us about a half hour to get to the cemetery and I want to stop for some flowers."

About forty-five minutes later, they were standing at Sonya's gravesite. They had placed the flowers near the headstone and Rusty had said a prayer.

"Would you mind if I spent some time alone with her?" he asked them. "It shouldn't be more than a few minutes."

Tanya looked at Jim and he could see the hurt in her eyes. She started to say something, but he put his fingers to his lips, took her hand and said, "We'll just take a little walk. There are some beautiful old historical sites ah want to show Tanya. Take as much time as ya need."

Jim led Tanya down the path until they were out of earshot.

"I am not playing second fiddle to my sister's ghost!" she blurted out emotionally.

Jim put his hands on her shoulders and looked her in the eyes sternly. "Ah'm goin' ta tell ya somethin' to help ya understand your husband a little betta'. What ah'm about ta tell ya is ta be kept in the strictest confidence. Ah kept a promise to you and Sonya that almost cost me mah best friend, now you must keep this confidence in return."

Tanya agreed and dried her eyes.

"Ta begin with, ah have known Rusty since he first joined the CIA over fifteen years ago. About six years ago, he was comin' off an assignment and was ta take a vacation, but ah had a situation that ah needed his help to settle."

Jim proceeded to tell Tanya about the whole situation with the East German operative that tried to kill him for bumping into him and about how he had introduced Sonya to Rusty at an Embassy social party scheduled during that time.

"For six years they had a love life and a life of love. Then Oc-

241

tober before last, Sonya went on an assignment with the Polish government that was ta last a number of months and she wouldn't be able to spend any time with him. She told him ta take his vacation with his family and ta enjoy Christmas with them. Grudgingly he did. Two weeks later she came ta me and said she was bein' followed and didn't know what ta do. Ah said ah could call Sundance for her and get him out here, but she said no. Ah gave her a two inch .38 special, since she didn't normally carry a gun and so didn't have one right then. Ah also had another agent follow her for a while, but he stopped when things seemed ta have quieted down.

"The next part of the story ah got from other sources. It seems that the Black Raven followed her to a secluded part of the city, where he approached her to obtain some type of information (ah now believe that ta be your late husband's formula). He was gettin' physically abusive, but she didn't know anythin' about it and kicked the Raven in the groin to get away. She started runnin' but he backhanded her, knockin' her about eight feet. She grabbed her .38 and put two slugs into his left side, but he returned the fire and hit her in the heart. She died instantly.

"Rusty feels that if he had been there, he could have saved her life. Her death broke that big man's heart so bad that if he hadn't had revenge ta live for, he probably wouldn't have bothered goin' on. He blames himself for not bein' there, but doesn't seem ta realize that the Raven would have waited until he wasn't around and would have accomplished the same dastardly deed.

"Rusty is spendin' his private time with Sonya hopin' that somehow, she might forgive him."

Suddenly there was a bright, beautiful light shining on Sonya's grave and the two of them seemed to be suspended in time. Rusty looked up and there was the twins' Guardian Angel. She was still so beautiful that she took his breath away.

"Sundance, I can feel your sorrow and pain. The one you loved is in a peaceful place and feels that there is no need for you to ask forgiveness, but grants it to you anyway also that you may find peace within yourself.

"Remember, Sundance, you have made me a promise that you must still keep. The twins are not yet of age and they still have a rough rocky path ahead of them. They will need you to help them to navigate that path safely."

"I have every intention of honoring that promise," Rusty said solemnly.

She smiled down at him and placed her hand on his head. He felt a strong bittersweet love flow through him and then she was gone. He felt as though a huge weight had been lifted from his heart. *I will never experience another feeling like that one as long as I live.*

Tanya and Jim rushed over to make sure that he was all right. He told them what the angel had said to him about Sonya being in a peaceful place and that the twins still had a rough path ahead of them.

"I never truly believed that story about the Guardian Angel," Tanya said. "It always seemed to incredible. I'll never doubt anything you say again. I love you and we'll all get through the rough path together."

"I love you too. Why don't we all go to lunch now. I know a great little restaurant that Sonya and I used to love going to."

The three of them headed back to the car in good spirits, looking forward to the rest of the day and the rest of their lives. It was a beautiful day.